Lock Down Publications and Ca$h
Presents

THE MURDER QUEENS 7

THEIR DEATH WAS INEVITABLE

Written By
Michael Gallon
and Rhynyia (Sexy Redd) Santiago

First Edition 2025

Printed in the United States of America

Lock Down Publications
P.O. Box 944
Stockbridge, GA 30281
www.lockdownpublications.com

Like our page on Facebook: Lock Down Publications
www.facebook.com/lockdownpublications.ldp

Stay Connected with Us!

Text **LOCKDOWN** to 22828 to stay up-to-date with new releases, sneak peaks, contests and more…

Like our page on Facebook:
Lock Down Publications

Join Lock Down Publications/The New Era Reading Group

Visit our website:
www.lockdownpublications.com

Follow us on Instagram:
Lock Down Publications

Email Us: We want to hear from you!

PROLOGUE

Rhynyia was awakened to sheer terror on Maria's face. Once she was informed of what was taking place, she sprinted to the cockpit. Miguel looked terrified when she told him to take the plane over the Bermuda Triangle. He told her that he couldn't put them in that type of danger.

"Well, if you won't, I will! Now move out of my gotdamn way!" Rhynyia shouted as she took control of the giant bird in the sky. Moments later they had lost the police helicopter and thought they were in the clear, when out of nowhere came a bolt of lighting that struck one of the plane's engines. "What was that?" she shouted to a frightened Miguel who was seated in the other pilot's seat.

His head quickly went to where the loud noise had come from. When he turned back around, he shouted, "We just lost an engine!"

Rhynyia began to struggle with the steering wheel of the plane, but her attempts were futile as she lost control. "We're going down! We're going down!" she screamed as she and the crew prepared for the worst. "Lord, help us!" were the last words they all heard as she tried her best to gain control of the plane.

Chapter 1
A Few Minutes 2 Late!

As the ambulance pulled up to the old wreckage that resembled a warehouse, my stomach began to turn as I stood there outside of the vehicle. Afraid of what may have already happened to my superior team of ladies known as the Murder Queens. At first, I thought about calling my sister and telling her that something awful had went down and that all of the ladies were dead somewhere deep off inside Jacksonville, Florida. And to think, we all were just a few minutes too late. I guess it was fitting for the women to have been murdered inside the same place where just a few weeks prior Chyna and this new white chick in the group had been tricked and left here to fend for themselves. Now the rest of my elite team of women were here, left for dead.

All of this ran throughout my mental. It wasn't until Rhynyia slapped me on the shoulder and uttered, "C'mon, man. Let's go!"

I quickly changed my mind as we were the first ones to jump out of the vehicle with Firstborn and Natasha following right behind us— their weapons drawn, ready to fire at whatever or whomever crossed our path. My head was still a bit cloudy about the scene as I looked over to my brother and said, "Hey, you go around back and see if you can get a number on how many guys are inside."

"Yeah, and whatever you do, don't get yourself killed," Natasha recited as she kissed him passionately on his lips, almost as if he wasn't going to come back.

"Whatever you do, nigga, come back!" I spoke; assurance laced in my voice.

"Don't you two worry. I have too much life ahead of me to go out right now," he replied as he winked at the both of us, then crouched under the window of the building, treading softly while he went around back, not knowing what may be back there waiting on him.

"Damn, Michael, I thought that you said that you were the one who went into the Army?" Rhynyia said to me as she observed the way my brother moved.

"I was. Why do you say that?"

"Because with the way his ass crept behind the building, one would think that his ass had some military training in his background," she said with a half smirk on her face.

"Girl, if you only knew. That nigga has done nothing but steal his entire life. That's probably how he used to run up in people's houses and steal everything of value," I uttered as I thought back to when I had heard that one hot and sunny day.

My brother's aunt and mother, along with some other family members, were seated in one of their air-conditioned rooms watching television. They were so in tune with what was on the screen that no one noticed that the air conditioner that they had stuck off in their window was being tampered with. Before anyone knew it, my gotdamn brother had snatched the air conditioner out of the window and was walking down the road with it up under his arm. Thirty minutes later, he had sold it for a twenty-piece of crack rock. So, as you see, my brother was a real piece of work.

I was still somewhat dazed and confused by the day's events as I began searching as well for any clues about what may have happened to the ladies, mainly trying to see if Nicole was shot up or somewhere barely clinging on to her dear life from an apparent bullet.

"Michael," Rhynyia whispered as loud as she could without being heard.

"Yeah?" I whispered back as I turned to stare at her and her sister.

"I think you need to come over here and check this shit out!" she said with an obscure look about her face.

I nonchalantly stood up from where I was, barely being able to walk through all the waste material that was located out front of the structure. With my head held down, I dimly walked over to where Rhynyia and her sister stood, looking over what I had already assumed to be Nicole's lethargic body lying there, since the last thing I heard was the gunshot and then her phone went dead.

"Michael! Hurry your ass up! You're not going to believe this shit!" she said while recklessly waving her hand as if for me to get to where her and her sister stood as quick as possible. The closer I approached, the weaker my body became with the thought of how things had spiraled out of control like this so fucking fast. If only I would have stayed my black ass home instead of going over to Puerto Rico with Rhynyia, maybe all of this could have been prevented.

With the vague facial expressions Rhynyia and Natasha held, it only reinforced my thought of it being the body of my special lil' Lady who we all knew as Nicole on that cold, damp ground with a bullet to the back of her cranium. As soon as my eyes came in contact with what looked like a dead corpse, I threw up everything that I had eaten that day and any other day before that. The horrific sight of the person laying there was too hideous to bear as half of the person's head was blown completely off with their right eye still being partly open as if they never got the chance to see what was coming.

Just as I had stopped throwing up and wiping my mouth clean of vomit and saliva, Rhynyia looked up at me with her weapon hanging down at her waist and said, "Damn, son, don't tell me that you can't stand to bear such a gruesome sight like this?" She still had that same smirk on her face as she continued. "Wait until you see what my sister and I are about to do to them brothers inside!"

Chapter 2
Their Ass!

She was standing there looking at me with a devilish smirk on her face as I looked at her and sputtered, "Damn, Rhynyia, you like to see shit like this, I see," while still wiping my mouth and taking a deep sigh of relief that it wasn't Nicole who was laying there dead on the ground with a bullet in her head.

"Whatever, Michael. Grab your fucking testicles and act like the man I know you are! Because it's about to go down in the dirty, my nigga!"

I casually looked back at her, holding a smile on my face. "Rhynyia, must I remind your diabolical, twisted-minded ass that I saw shit like this every day while over in Desert Storm, fighting for this country! So maybe you should grab your nice plump ass titties and follow me!"

Her sister stood firm as she slid back the chamber on her weapon, letting me know that it was ready to fire. "Enough of the chit-chatting! Let's do this shit!" she said as she crouched under the smeared, brown-stained window of the warehouse.

But just as we were about to do our thing and follow behind her ass, Firstborn emerged from behind the warehouse, yelling, "Hey, Baby Boy! Look who I found behind the warehouse!"

Her beautiful smile and gleaming face gave me a slight bit of hope of rescuing the others as she said. "Hello, guys. It's nice to see that y'all finally made it to the party!"

I was the first one to approach her. "Nicole, girl I thought that you took a bullet to the noggin. I heard the gunshots and then your phone went dead."

"Yeah, I know. That was all due to me putting a few holes in your boy Jimmy Shit-Face McGriff's head right here!" she said as she pointed to the lifeless body of one of the goons that was supposed to be watching the outside of the warehouse, sprawled out on the ground.

"Damn, did you have to do the man like that?" I asked with a skeptical look on my face.

"I had to. Caught his ass slipping, trying to walk up on some free pussy and ass. So, I had to blast the fool!"

"Damn, look how half of the poor man's head is here and the other portion, only God knows where it's at?" Firstborn chimed in.

"Oh, my bad fellas. Was I supposed to ask his ass where he wanted me to shoot him before I did?" she asked as a smirk appeared on her face.

"Hey, you, don't mind them. Michael has been a bit cranky ever since we left the island. So you're okay, I see?" Rhynyia asked as they embraced one another for a brief moment. Once they let go, Rhynyia stood back to give Nicole a good look over.

"Yeah, chick, I'm good. You know a true Murder Queen never dies!"

I was over to the side, just happy to see my girl again. This is when I took a deep breath and theanked the Almighty up above for her safety and asked for the safety of the others while staring at how they were interacting since they hadn't spoken to one another since the shooting a few days ago, back at the house.

Nicole then looked over at me with a wink of her right eye, and said, "It's about five guys inside with our ladies all tied up, looking like they are about to do some real awful shit to their ass!"

***

Meanwhile, ducked off inside the warehouse, Strawberry told me later that Marquise had his boys tie up the girls as he yelled over to his partner Ouzi— a local hometown hero who had a scholarship to play football down in Miami. But after he found himself sitting on the bench the very first year, he decided that being a local drug dealer and part time do-boy would fancy his lifestyle more nicely.

"Alright, my dude, what's next?" Ouzi yelled as he stood, waiting on his orders.

"Man, strip them hoes butt ass naked. We're about to have ourselves a fucking orgy up in this muthafucka right before we kill their ass like they killed my baby brother and partner!" Marquise voiced as spittle flew from his mouth.

"Hold on, don't you forget that pretty ass nigga that you sent! What was his name again?" Mignon yelled as she stared death right in the eyes. "Oh, now I remember. His name was Death Certificate! Yeah, that's what his name was."

Marquise stood there with fire in his eyes as he grunted. "Fuck you, bitch. Keep running your fuck-ass mouth before we all fuck you in the ass last!"

She just gazed back at him while Carlos pulled the tape off of Punkin's thin lips. The first thing his short ass yelled was, "Man, fuck that! Someone pull this long ass play dick out of my fucking ass!" He then fell back down, due to him laying down all day, causing his legs to be weak. His anemic looking body fell hard to the floor, making a thunderous thud as it landed.

"What the hell, lil' ass nigga? Your black ass hands are fucking free. You can take that shit out of your asshole your-damn-self!" Stank D yelped as he went to unzip his pants in front of a naked Strawberry. Stank D, who had met up with Marquise earlier in the day, was the last goon invited to join the party. The brother stood around six foot even, weighing two hundred and ten pounds, with a low fade haircut that he adorned on his rectangular-shaped head. He was from Lakeland, Florida and was only up for the weekend when he heard that the Florida Hot Girls were in town.

"Yo, man, come here, I'll pull that long, nice, fat, black, thick dick out of your ass with my teeth! I mean my hand," Flash said as he limped over to where Punkin lay with his dildo still plunged up his ass as if it wasn't even there.

Punkin looked back at him while still laying there with a crazy ass unit on his face and shouted, "Man, stay your gay ass from around me, punk ass muthafucka! I knew that your ass was gay!" Punkin was still naked and feeling violated for having his virgin asshole violated by a twelve-inch dildo all day.

"Damn, if we knew that Flash was a Flame Thrower we would have placed Punkin's butt naked ass in front of him, so he could have smelt his lil' stanking ass all day."

"Fuck you, Strawberry!" Punkin yelled as he backed himself into a corner then, frantically trying to remove the painful object from his asshole.

Marquise was standing by Mignon, staring at the beauty of her naked body and wasn't trying to hear what was going on between the others while Stank D was standing up in front of Strawberry, saying to her, "I'm gonna kill your big-headed ass for sticking that play dick so far up my lil' homie's ass that he can taste it in his mouth. But first, I'm gonna fuck you in that wide, fat ass of yours!"

Strawberry farted, then uttered, "You can do what you like, but let me warn your dumb ass. I haven't shitted in three whole days. So, you know I'm going to shit all over you when you stick that lil' ass dick of yours inside my wide, fat ass, my nigga!"

Chapter 3
Pst-pst-pst!

Stank D stared at ole Berry as if she was a hundred-dollar steak dinner, then uttering the words, "Whatever, Trick, shut the hell up! Matter of fact, your pretty red ass is about to show me how you hoes eat the dick off of the bone, right-fucking-now!"

As soon as he finished his sentence, the rest of the guys with Marquise all began taking off their clothes with the deadly intentions of sodomizing all the ladies they had tied up, while my crew and I were getting ready to storm down the door and start blasting on them wild and crazy ass brothers.

We were just about to bum rush the door when the one guy they called Flash ran across the floor screaming, "With all of this naked ass up in here, I don't ever want to go the fuck home!"

"What did that nigga just yell?" I turned to ask my brother.

His head was shaking when he replied, "Hell if I know, but whatever it was, I want no part of it."

Marquise, meanwhile, had just pulled Mignon's beautiful legs apart and was about to enter her tight, bare vagina as she looked at him in his cold-hearted, red-colored eyes. The poor darling had a lone tear streaking down her face as she whispered, "So you're just going to take what you can't have, right?"

He coughed up some greenish looking phlegm and spat at her feet. "Hell yeah, bitch! You hoes took what wasn't yours when you all decided to kill my baby brother and his partner, right?"

"Don't forget Death Certificate," she voiced as she cut a wicked smirk in his direction.

"Yeah, his ass, too."

"Well, I hope that you enjoy this pussy because it's the last piece of ass that you'll ever get before you die!" She then spat back in his face, hitting him right across his thick, crusty-looking lips.

He then took his right hand and wiped the spit off inside of his mouth, tasting it, then saying, "Bitch, you have a mean ass talk game for a trick who is about to get fucked, right before taking a bullet to the head!"

She just smiled as he stood there stroking his manhood, trying to get right before he penetrated her. Mignon saw what he was doing and started chuckling to herself, then smiling as the grotesque-looking brother doing himself. The brother was actually jacking himself off before he could enter her beautiful, shaven vagina.

"What's so fucking funny, bitch?" he asked as he never missed a stroke.

"What's funny is that your baby brother's dick was way bigger than yours!" she spat.

Waaaaaap! He slapped her so fucking hard that blood shot out of her bottom lip while he snarled at her for what she had just said. "It don't matter, bitch. This is the last dick that you're gonna see any-damn-way. Because just as soon as I fuck you at least three times, I'm gonna turn your ass around and then fuck you in that fine, red ass of yours, dead or alive!"

She still had the half smirk on her face as she uttered, "It don't matter. Your dick is so damn small that I won't feel it anyway!"

His face became enraged as he stood there holding all four inches of his short, thick manhood in his fat ass hands.

"Not if I can help it, homie!" *Pst-pst-pst!* We burst through the door with Firstborn firing off rounds in the direction of Marquise who was caught completely off guard, butt naked with a silly ass facial expression.

My brother's first shot tore off the man's right kneecap as the big fella fell hard to the floor screaming out in pain. "Ahhh shit! What the fuck?"

The other two shots flew past his head, due to him falling aimlessly to the floor, causing my brother to miss his big ass.

His homie Stank D was as lucky as he was, all due to Rhynyia hitting the brother four times in his back with her 9-millimeter. The bullets were piercing as his body seemed to jerk every time one of the hollow points ripped a hole into him. "Damn, bitch!" he shouted as he fell face-first to the cement floor, slightly breathing, now trying to hold on for dear life.

"'Bout damn time! What took you hoes so long to get here?" Strawberry yelled as she opened her eyes to see Rhynyia coming her way.

"We here now, bitch!" Rhynyia shouted back as she untied her hands.

Just as she got free, she uttered, "Let me hold that."

"What?"

"The gun, Rhynyia, the gun!" Strawberry took Rhynyia's 9-millimeter Glock.

Pst-pst-pst! Strawberry kicked Stank D over onto his back and fired four precise shots directly into his face. "Good luck with an open casket funeral," she spat as she spit on the dead man's face.

"Seriously?" Rhynyia asked as she stood there looking at her stark-naked friend.

"Hell yeah! That son of a bitch was still breathing."

Rhynyia looked at the dead corpse then back at ole Berry. "If you ask me, looks like overkill, Strawberry."

"What the fuck ever. Fuck him and his sorry ass life!" she sputtered as she looked back up at Rhynyia.

Over to the right of the warehouse, their partner Carlos was trying to sprint for the back door when Natasha hit him directly in the back of his head with two shots that, believe it or not, went through the same exact hole. All I could do was stand there and shake my head at the Sharpshooter All one could hear was a loud noise as his body fell lifeless to the cement floor. On his way to hell, his body knocked over a few barrels of old newspapers.

"Dammit!" she yelled.

"What? You hit your target," I said as I stood next to her, wondering what was wrong with that.

"I meant to hit him in his legs, not that big ass head of his."

"Girl, are you serious?" I asked, trying not to smile.

"Yes, but I knew that you probably wanted to talk to him before he took a first-class flight to the next world."

"Hell nah! Always remember this when it comes to killing someone. Dead people can't talk," I voiced as we all looked over, seeing Marquise, Punkin, and Flash still alive, with their manhood in their hands.

Marquise was rolling over on the ground when he looked up at Punkin and asked him. "Who in the fuck is that pretty muthafucka, standing beside that Nicole bitch?"

"That's the nigga who them hoe's work for, the one I told you that was over in Puerto Rico," Punkin muttered as he just sat there, knowing that his young life was about to be over.

Meanwhile, Rhynyia and her sister were busy untying the ladies and assisting them with putting back on their attire when Nicole stepped into Punkin's face. "Nigga, how many times do I have to tell your dumb ass that we're not hoes!" She then slapped the shit out of his ass, kicking him in his stomach at the same damn time.

Blood and snot began to ooze out of his mouth as he leaned over, clutching his stomach, crying and wishing that he would've never got himself involved with what Marquise had planned. "Man, listen, we can work this shit out so there doesn't have to be any more bloodshed here on this early Sunday morning!" he voiced with sweat and tears furiously running down his face.

"Yeah, I wish that we could have, but no, you had to bring my ladies here and strip them of their dignity," I replied while brandishing my Four Nickel at bay.

"Nah, Mike, this nigga wanted to rape us then kill every one of us!" Strawberry yelled as she walked up on Punkin and punched him in his stomach again.

"Hold on, bruh. Who is the nigga standing over there with that black thing hanging out of his ass?" Firstborn asked out loud while having a fucked up unit on his face.

"Hell if I know!" I quickly said.

"That's their gay ass partner, Flash!" Entyce muttered as she picked up a gun from the floor, turned it on Flash, then unloaded a full clip into his gay ass, causing his body to wildly jerk with every painful round that entered into his tall, lean, sickly body.

Rhynyia had to actually snatch the gun from her hand as Entyce stood there still trying to fire the weapon after the clip had been emptied. "Entyce, calm down, girl! It's not that serious!" Rhynyia uttered as she slowly pulled the gun away from her fingers, still holding tightly to the trigger of the weapon.

At that moment was when I got the distinct feeling that Entyce had seen enough killing. And it wouldn't be long until the minute she would tell me that she had had enough.

Chapter 4

Any Other Way!

Entyce then looked into the face of Rhynyia before she said. "Yes, it is, but these bitch-made niggas were going to rape us then kill us! I had to have my revenge because I was too close to facing death, Sexy Redd!" She then fell into her arms and began sobbing uncontrollably.

Just by witnessing the sight of her crying like that, I knew then that my girl had seen too much killing in her young life. With the murder rate those young women were having at that time and moment, the poor darling had seen more killing in her life than the average soldier did in his entire military career. Like I said, it would only be a matter of time before she would reconsider her job choice in life.

Shaking my head, I looked over at Marquise laying there on the floor, bleeding profusely from his open leg wound. "You see what you have caused one of my girls to do? Now look over there at your gay ass homie, over there filled with holes all over his dead body."

"And not to mention, with a big, long ass dildo hung up his ass, Baby Boy," Firstborn said with a fiendish smirk on his face.

"Yo, c'mon, Mike, man. Please let us go and I promise I'll forget that this shit ever happened!" Marquise begged.

"Yeah right, partner, you must think that I'm stupid or something. Just as soon as we all leave, you and what's left of your small ass crew will be down in Orlando, looking for us."

He was shaking his head frantically, even muttering, "No-no-no! I promise, Mike, we won't come bothering you guys at all. Just please let us go!"

"Now your big, black ass knows that we can't have you niggas hunting us down like dogs and then killing us in the streets?" I uttered, heart really bleeding for my man who had death and bitterness all in his eyes. Tears and snot were flowing down the man's face as he tried to assure me that him and his boy's life should be spared as the girls and I heard what sounded like sirens in the distance.

"Sounds like they are a few miles away. If we're going to do something, we need to do it now!" Natasha yelled with a little urgency in her voice.

This is when Rhynyia looked at me with those praline brown eyes of hers before she yelled out to Mignon. "Murder Queens for Life, bitch! This is what we do!"

Moments later, Strawberry, Rhynyia, Mignon, Nicole, Tameia and your girl Entyce were all standing there unloading their weapons of choice into the bodies of the young gentlemen who were about to rob them of their dignity, pride and life while Firstborn and I walked outside to get ready for a quick getaway.

"Listen, get back to the airport with Rhynyia and her sister. Get the Yayo and then get home safely as you can," I said as he reached out to me.

"Mike, how, my nigga? I have no vehicle!" His eyes were wide as fuck as he stood there staring at me.

"Oh shit! My bad, hold on, let me make a quick call!" I said to him as I went for my phone. Moments later, I was on my phone thanking the Lady. "Alright, you're good to go. Once you all get back to the airport, there is a Cadillac Escalade waiting for Rhynyia to pick up for you."

"Good thinking, bruh, 'cause you know my ass don't have any driver license," he uttered as he smiled at me. This was the first time since we had left Rhynyia's place that me and this rock headed nigga had even really spoke to one another in the manner in which we did.

"Damn, my nigga, so all this time that your black ass has been driving, you had no license?" I asked as I stared at his ass.

"Yep, not one at all!"

"Boy, you be taking some chances, don't you?"

"Hell yeah. I wouldn't be me if I didn't," he said back to me.

Come to think about it, hell I didn't have any driver license either. Not to mention that at that time in my life, my black ass had three warrants out for me and was just about to be placed on Orlando's top list of people running from the long arms of the law. Don't worry though, I'm about to tell you all about how that happened for a smooth brother like myself.

The sounds of the sirens were getting closer as my brother and I stood there talking and planning our escape route. I was just about to step back inside of the warehouse to check on the ladies.

"Look at my baby brother. You're a grown man now!"

"I've been a grown man for a long time, Firstborn. You have just always treated me like a lil' brother," I voiced as Rhynyia and the ladies started emerging from inside the building without a drop of sweat or blood on their bodies.

"Bae, we left quite a mess inside. I'm pretty sure that someone will clean it up. Right now we have to get out of here, real quick."

"You're right. Listen, when you all get back to the airport, there should be a rental truck registered in your name."

"Why? Where am I driving it to?" she asked, still looking cute as ever to me.

"You're not. It's for my brother. Once he loads up the Yayo, his ass is going to drive back home to Madison, Florida."

"Okay. Anything else?" she asked.

"Yes, make sure you call me as soon as you guys get over the Atlantic and remember I love you!" I versed, sirens getting closer.

"I love you too, Michael, and so does your unborn son. So don't you go and get yourself killed, trying to be someone's hero. Bye, Michael Vallentino," she said to me as the three of them jumped back into the ambulance. Before the doors closed, she stuck her head out. "Alright, ladies, until I return. You bitches be good and take care of my muthafucking man! And please don't make me come back and fuck one of y'all up for fucking his black ass!" With all of that said, she slammed the door of the ambulance and then slammed her hand on it twice, alerting the driver to pull off.

Mignon looked over at Nicole. "She was talking to your black ass!"

"Whatever, chick. Let's get the hell out of here!"

"Yeah, she's right." I voiced.

"I know that's right, because for a moment there I thought that we were all just going to wait for the cops to come and ask us what in the hell happened here?" Nicole said as she looked at me and then gave me one of her cute ass half smiles.

"I know that's right. Let's bounce!" Mignon voiced as she got into the driver's seat of the truck she had rented.

"Mike, let's go! The cops will be here any minute!" Strawberry yelled to me as she climbed in the front seat of my truck while I stood there, looking back inside the warehouse at the array of dead bodies that my ladies had left behind.

Damn, what else are these damn ladies capable of doing? I asked myself as I went to get into the driver's seat of my truck. Whatever it was or might be I was sure as hell about to find out once I got back to Black Magic to pick up the rest of my Florida Hot Girls. Just as I sat down, I had to take a deep sigh of relief, realizing that it must have been those dead guys' time to die. In other words: *their death was inevitable.*

Chapter 5
Watch Out!

Just as soon as we pulled out of the parking lot is when I turned to Strawberry and asked her, "So you all just had to make Tameia a member of your group, huh?"

"It's a long story, Mike. Remind me to tell you when we all get back to the house," she said as she stared up ahead. I guess she was watching how Mignon was whipping the rental truck.

"Whatever," was all I said as I followed right behind my girl who made a sharp turn onto Washington Street.

We were all trying to get as far away from the crime scene as possible. At the rate of speed that she was driving, I was sure that we would get pulled over by the local police as we both sped down Washington Street, doing at least eighty-five miles per hour.

Then out of nowhere, we sped right past a convoy of police cruisers, all headed for the warehouse we had just come from. My head quickly snapped back, looking to make sure they didn't turn around to follow us. Once I seen that they were preoccupied with something more appealing, I reached for my phone and yelled straight through our two-way devices.

"Mignon, please slow that big ass truck down. We do not need to get pulled over!"

She swiftly came back with, "I got this, Mike. Just hold on! I need to get us as far away as possible. And besides, we still have to get to the club to pick up the rest of the girls!"

"Okay, Mignon, you're the boss!" I shouted back as I placed my phone down to hear Strawberry.

"I'm glad that you guys made it in time to save our black ass!" she stated.

"Yeah, me, too. If we would have gotten there a minute too late, there is no telling what would've happened to you beautiful young ladies."

"You do have a point their Mike, because I don't know what we would've done if you, Rhynyia and your brother wouldn't have made it in time," Strawberry said to me as she looked back into the rearview mirror, making sure that there wasn't any cops following behind us."

"Didn't I just say something like that, ole silly ass girl?"

"My bad, you probably did, Mike. By the way, who was that other cute Puerto Rican chick with you guys?" she asked as she looked over at me.

"That was Rhynyia's sister, Natasha. It seems as though she's one of you guys as well," I uttered as I wiped sweat from my brow.

"What do you mean by one of us? What, is she a dancer, too?"

"No, girl, she's one of the Murder Queens as well."

"Nah, not that pretty, innocent-looking girl?" she asked with a surprised look on her face.

"Yep, that she is. Hell, she was the first one to jump into action as soon as we got there. So make sure that you thank her if y'all ever see each other again," I recited as Mignon made a right turn onto Beaver Street, headed straight for the club, leaving me thinking to myself of what I had just said. Deep down in my soul I knew that the only way that they would see her sister again would be if my brother fucked up their father's Yayo and money. Or maybe if I was lucky enough to one day fulfill my obligations and really did get the chance to marry Rhynyia.

Moments later, both trucks were pulling up near a curb somewhere in close proximity to the club. Strawberry and myself jumped out of my truck and got into the truck with Mignon and the others, just as they were removing their torn clothing that they had on.

As Mignon slid her shirt up over her head, she dully turned to the back seat and said, "Alright, ladies, no one is to know nothing. I mean nothing about where we were or what we were doing. So, keep your mouth shut!"

Damn, since I had been gone, it seemed as though Mignon had really taken over my group. She was talking to the ladies as if I wasn't even there. I was so intrigued by her tone and actions that I didn't even notice a quiet Nicole seated beside me with her head resting on the door of the rental. "Hey, are you okay?" I asked her, feeling sorry for her since knowing what she had been going through. Not to mention with her still carrying our child.

"Yes, Michael, I'm fine. What about you, Mister? Are you okay?" she asked me as she slowly lifted her head and gave me a nonchalant looking smile.

"I couldn't be better now that I'm here sitting amongst family and friends, Nicole." She then eased up in the seat. "Well, since you put it like that, Michael, there is something of importance that I need to tell you." I lazily turned to face her as she softly began to speak. "I don't know how to tell you this, but—"

I stopped her and placed my index finger over her soft, wet lips. "Listen, you have nothing to worry about, my dear. I'm going to be there for you and my unborn seed, no matter what." This is when she sat there motionless as she slowly began to cry hot tears. At that moment I didn't know if she was crying tears of joy or just simply crying. All I knew was that Mignon had the rented SUV sitting off to the side of Black Magic facing oncoming traffic, when all of a sudden I heard Strawberry screaming at the top of her lungs.

"Oh my God, watch out!"

Chapter 6
Deadly Intruder!

Little Breanna sat on the floor, motionless, screaming and crying out loud at what she had just witnessed. It was her loud screams that brought Sharon back from the point of no return. Her weapon of choice was still smoldering as she stood over the deceased body of her violent assailant. Once she wiped her face of the terror, she searched the floor in sheer panic, looking for her cell phone so that she could call 911 and alert them of the intruder that she had just shot and killed at point blank range.

The operator answered her call on the first ring. "911, what's your emergency?" the calm voice of the operator said.

"Yes, I would like to report that I just shot an intruder!" Sharon hysterically said into the phone while her young daughter continued crying in the background.

"Okay, ma'am! Are you okay?"

"Yes, I'm going to need an ambulance and the police immediately!"

"No problem, ma'am. We do have an officer enroute to you as we speak. So please stay on the line with me until one arrives."

"Yes, ma'am," she said as she went to pick up her daughter. "It's okay, baby, stop crying; mommy is alright, okay?"

Breanna nodded as she sat in her mother's arms, staring down at the deceased man sprawled out on the floor. Not wanting her daughter to witness this, she walked into the kitchen with Breanna. She wanted to pour her something to drink, hoping that this would calm her young daughter down. But just as she was about to pour her something to drink, one of the neighbors happened to walk through the open front door.

"Oh my goodness, what happened?" the neighbor asked, shock written all over her face.

"I have no idea. I was on the phone with my mother when I thought that I heard someone creeping around out front. The phone went dead when I heard a knock at my front door. When I answered it, the man on the floor lunged through the door at me. The next thing I knew, I was blasting two rounds at him, catching him directly in his!" Just as soon as she gave her short story of what happened, the first responding officer arrived.

"Oh my, you must be scared half to death?" her neighbor asked as she placed her hands over her nosy ass chest.

"Somewhat. I'll be okay just as long as his ass is fucking dead!" Sharon recited as the first officer walked through the door of her home.

"Ma'am," the operator said through the phone.

"Yes." Sharon answered.

"The officer is there now, right?"

"Yes, ma'am. He just arrived."

"Good. He will assist you now. The ambulance should be there soon."

"Thank you, ma'am," she replied as she prepared to hang up the phone. Sharon then placed her phone into her pocket and started explaining to the officer what had happened while members of the police department began arriving on the scene.

While one of the officers was asking Sharon questions on what had transpired, the other officer was the one who called over his fellow officers. "Hey, Rick, you might want to call this one in for me!" Officer Bryan said as he kneeled to place a sheet over the intruder's badly burned face. Officer Bryan

Richards had been on the force for at least three years and was damn good at what he called his dream job. He had desires and wants just like his father, who had been on the force ever since he was a lad.

As a bright-eyed young man, Officer Bryan Richards sat at home each day, waiting to hear the stories of what his father's day had been like. He began to play back all the good days and bad ones of what his detective father had told him. Those days and stories had been what had caused young Bryan to want to walk in his father's footsteps. But tonight and every other day after this one right here would become just faded memories for him. Because all of that was about to change after officer Bryan Richards walked into the home of Ms. Conoly and saw the intruder's body sprawled out on the floor. Dead from two precise rounds placed off inside his hairy ass chest. For the intruder was none other than his father, Lt. Richards.

***

As Sharon sat there explaining what had happened, half of the police force had emerged at her place of residence with questions and concerns of their own. Her place was in a frenzy as news reporters and her neighbors all converged outside of her house, trying to find out what had caused one of their most decorated officers to act out the way he did.

Meanwhile, Firstborn, Rhynyia and her sister Natasha had just made it back to the hangar, where Miguel and his small crew were waiting on their return.

Rhynyia was the first one out of the ambulance, shouting at Firstborn as she turned to him, "Alright, Firstborn, you have at least a thirty-minute window, so let's hurry up and load that shit up! We have to get in the air within the next twenty minutes!"

She and her sister had just made it up the steps of the private jet when Maria stopped her at the entrance. "Princess,

I'm afraid that we don't have that long. I just heard over the police scanner that the police are on their way to inspect a plane that looks suspicious!"

"Are you sure they were talking about this particular plane?" Rhynyia asked with a frantic look about her face.

"Yes, Princess, I'm positive! They even said what hangar we are located at!" Maria told her, fright laced in her voice.

"Okay, so how long do you think we have here?" Rhynyia asked her as my brother and Natasha were already packing up the Yayo.

"It looks like a good ten minutes, Princess." Maria had a look of sheer panic and concern on her face.

"Miguel, start the engines!" Rhynyia shouted to Miguel, then turned back to the open door of the plane. "Firstborn, we have to do this expeditiously. The police are already on their way here!"

The engines came on as my brother and the rest of them worked frantically, trying to load up the Yayo. It wasn't until the entire crew of the plane formed a human chain and then started passing the Yayo to a waiting Firstborn. Deeply embedded in my brother's mind was the thought and reality of what if he and the rest of them were caught with that much product? What would they all do? He knew damn well that his black ass wasn't going to take the charge for all that weight.

Like he had stated previously, before we took off for Puerto Rico, he was already a three-time felon. One more strike would certainly mean life behind bars. Especially with all the weight they had on that plane. That's exactly why all the way up until this very day, I just couldn't figure out why my brother, my only brother, agreed to sell that much product and put his life in danger like that. If only I had the chance to ask him why, maybe I would know the answer to that simple question.

Chapter 8
Hangar 22!

They were all up against the clock. I'm pretty sure that not one of them wanted to be caught with that much product on their hands. So, they had all of their father's precious products packed within minutes.

The last of the yayo had just been packed when Rhynyia looked at my brother and asked him, "Are you going to be okay?"

He looked back at her as he climbed into the truck, ready to get on the road headed to Madison, Florida. "Hey, if it's something meant for me to do, then you best believe that I'm gonna do it!"

She cut a half smile at his slick mouth ass, even though she was still somewhat upset at him for agreeing to push his product. "Whatever, Firstborn. Get your black ass out of here before you get us all screwed up with all of that White Girl that you now have with you, Tony Montana."

"Tony who?" he asked with a bewildered look on his face.

"Tony Montana, Firstborn. What, don't tell me that you never saw the movie Scarface?" she asked.

He scratched his bald head for a minute, then looked back at her, saying, "Nope, don't think that I have."

She laughed, lightly. "Boy, get yo' crazy ass out of here!" She still held the half smile on her face as Natasha stood in the way of him driving away.

"What now?" he asked her as he stuck his head out of the window of the truck.

She then slowly walked around to the driver's side and softly spoke. "Please don't make me come hunt your black ass down, Firstborn."

"Never that, sweetheart. I'll see you soon." He smiled.

"We'll see," she said to him as he drove away, headed for Interstate Ten with thirty kilos of some of the world's purest cocaine. As he drove out of the airport, he flew right past five police cruisers headed to question the pilot of the luxury plane in hangar twenty-two.

***

As the high-powered twin-engine jet hurried down the runway without clearance, Rhynyia yelled to the pilot while taking off her black attire, "Alright, Miguel, take us home!" She then walked to the rear of the plane so that she could wipe away the aftereffects of the night's escapade. She was just about to walk past her sister who was seated, gazing out the window, looking like she was about to cry. I guess after seeing my brother drive away with her father's product and her virgin heart. "Everything will be okay, Natasha. Trust me on that. One thing about Michael is that he has never let me down," she said to her sister as she held out her hand to help comfort her.

"It's not Michael that I'm worried about, big sis. It's his wild and crazy ass brother." They both looked at one another, then smiled together as the plane ascended into the dark of the early morning skies.

The officers of the local police department stood outside of their patrol cars looking into the dark sky, watching the beautiful luxury jet fly away. "Damn, there goes our chance for a fucking promotion, Officer Brown!" the short, fat, white, redneck officer said to his middle-aged black partner.

"Yep, maybe next time!" Officer Brown replied as he smiled, thinking, *I'm glad they got away!*

You see, Officer Brown had been on the force for at least twelve years, and in that short period of time the young black brother had witnessed so much police brutality on the black community from his department that he was actually glad that whomever it was on the plane had got away.

"Yep, another brother done got away. Good for him. Lord knows what would've happened to him if he had dope on that plane," Officer Brown said out loud as he went to get back into the patrol car with his racist ass partner.

"What was that, Brown?" Officer Collier asked as he sat back down in the driver seat.

"Nothing, Boss. I didn't say anything there, Boss," Officer Brown uttered as he turned his head and smiled at the plane flying away.

The Plane was far away and out of sight when Rhynyia came back to her seat and sat down. She casually leaned her head back and was about to doze off when Maria walked up to her.

"Will you be in need of anything else, Princess?"

Rhynyia coyly smiled back at her. "No, my dear lady. Wake me up ten minutes before we land, please."

"Yes. No problem, Princess."

***

On the other side of the city, the white and black chromed semi-tractor trailer that was hauling frozen foods for Publix Grocery Stores just missed us by at least five feet. The driver of the truck probably never even noticed that he was about to cause an accident that neither I nor the ladies were prepared to endure. It was the outburst from Strawberry's sweet, sexy lips yelling at Mignon just as she did the very first time my brother rammed his rock-hard manhood deep inside of her tight ass vagina. Not to mention the driver of the truck was most likely a Meth Head— a drug that would help keep him awake on long, tiring trips back and forth from

Lakeland, Florida to Jacksonville, Florida as he was probably too busy filling up his decaying lungs with one of the world's least expensive drugs to manufacture. Nonetheless it was a very close call, because he probably would have killed us all right there on Beaver Street, that early mid-morning. After the intense moment, we all took a deep sigh of relief then thanked the Almighty up above for being pulled out of the jaws of death once again.

"Is everyone okay?" I asked the girls who were busy checking over their bodies for any marks from being tossed around the large SUV.

"Yes, we're all good, Mike," Mignon said to me as she crawled her lovely half naked body over the seat so that she could finish changing back into her attire that she had on when she dropped the girls off earlier. She plopped her tender ass right down in between me and Nicole, which made it difficult to hear Nicole when she called out to me.

"Mike?" A teary-eyed Nicole cried out to me as she attempted to place her head around Mignon.

"Yes, beautiful?"

Just as she was about to say something to me, Mignon placed the palm of her hand on Nicole's thigh and whispered to her. "Not now. Wait until later, Nicole. With everything that has transpired tonight, it would probably be better if you waited until all the smoke cleared."

"You're right. Thanks, chick."

I was trying to listen to what they were discussing amongst themselves, all while trying to make sense out of what Mignon kept Nicole from telling me. My complicated mind went to wondering what it was since this was the first time that I had even talked to Nicole since I left for Puerto Rico. Hell, I hadn't talked to her since that day we all got back, and I held the cookout for them over at my place. Moments later I was blowing the event off, once we all started getting out of the vehicle, especially as I watched how nice her ass looked in her outfit that she had on. One thing that I did happen to notice though, was that her stomach wasn't poking out as it was before I had left.

As they all walked up ahead of me, about to enter the club, I quickly called out to Mignon. "Hey, Mignon, hold up for a quick minute, please!"

She turned around and walked back to me while the rest of the ladies waited for us at the door. "Yeah, Mike? What's up?" she asked as if nothing had happened a few hours ago.

"What is eating your girl Nicole? Why is she acting like there is something wrong with her?" I asked Mignon as I placed my hand on her shoulder.

She looked at me, eyes gleaming back at me. "Mike, that's for you and Nicole to discuss. You know that I really don't like getting into anyone's business. Especially not when it comes between you and Nicole." She batted her eyelashes, then placed her head down.

I would be a fool not to notice that ever since the first time she was involved within my group at that moment I actually felt a certain type of way about her. And for just that brief second there, I thought that we were about to actually suck-face one another. But that sensation or moment was rudely interrupted when Suga Bear and Peekachu walked outside of the club screaming.

"Oh shit! Our muthafucking dawg is back! Hey, y'all! His black ass is back!" They screamed as me and the few ladies that were draped by my side walked to the front door of the club. At that very moment I can honestly say that my life meant nothing to me without my precious, adorable, exotic stable of beautiful women known as the world famous Florida Hot Girls.

Chapter 9
Street Clothes On!

We all walked inside the club as if we were famous. The crowd was oohing and awing as they saw the beautiful Murder Queens on my arm, who, to me, looked like professional strippers in their street clothes. In their club attire they were just as jaw-dropping. For the most part, I actually felt like I was on top of the world. But only if someone would have told me about the downfall of this lifestyle that I was living now, I would have thrown in the towel at my first opportunity to do so.

The music was nice, and the DJ had the club amped up with the artist Big Mike, singing his hit song *Having Thangs* as I was pointing at and speaking to the niggas who were all waving and shouting out my name, trying to speak to me since I had walked in the door of the club with five more badass, tantalizing Florida Hot Girls, who during their part time worked as professional hit women.

I could barely see through the establishment due to all of the cigarette, weed, and whatever else the patrons of the tiny establishment known as Black Magic— one of the most talked about in Jacksonville— were smoking on.

The sea of all the thick smoke filled the air in the already crowded club, which was packed from small wall to small ass wall. The girls and I fought our way to the back of the club. It had been a minute since I had been in the presence of such a large crowd without my brother watching my back. Now that he was back home to become one of Florida's most sought-after drug dealers, I would have to rely on my Murder Queens for my protection and safety. As we lazily walked throughout the club, I turned my head slightly to see Malik from the corner of my eye, standing behind the bar area, talking with his bartender. He must have sensed that some big-time celebrity had walked through the door of his club with the way the attendants were hooping and hollering.

That's when he looked up and witnessed me walking through the multitude of people and shouted out, "Yo, Mike! What's good, homie?" A crooked smile covered his face.

"Nothing much, Cool Breeze. Just glad to be back!" I replied while looking over at all of the girls I had working in his club.

I caught Chyna and Ms. Bad Ass Mo Money up on *Stage* as Mo Money saw me and cut a cute lil' grin over in my direction. She then blew me a kiss. I pretended to catch it in mid-air and then placed it inside of my tailor-fitted slacks. She then pointed down to the large quantity of money that laced the stage floor.

I yelled out to her and Chyna, "Damn, you two have enough money on the floor to buy some needy kids school clothes!"

"Whatever, Mike!" Chyna shouted back to me while having her gorgeous smile wrapped around her light skinned face.

"Damn, she was so fucking fine," I mumbled to myself.

"Hey, Mike."

I quickly turned my head to see where the cute voice came from and who it belonged to. When I fully turned around it was my girl Charlie B standing directly behind my ass. "Hello to you, Charlie B, with your fine, red ass," I said as I saw my girl Chazz off to the left of the club with three guys, all throwing nothing but nickel bags of weed at her ass. "Damn, Chazz, I don't take weed as my tip out fee!"

"Shut up, Mike! I have my tip out fee right here," she said to me as she smacked me across my face with her Crown Royal Bag.

I just smiled at her ass and continued to the back of the club with the ladies I had just come in the door with.

This lil' skinny, young thug looking nigga asked me, "Hey, are they dancing tonight?"

I looked back at the fella with a side smirk on my face. "Hell, I don't know. Why don't you ask them?"

Mignon leaned her head into the guy's chest as she whispered into his ear, "It all depends on how long your money is tonight, baby."

The young thug pulled out at least three bands of money wrapped in individual rubber bands.

She turned to Entyce and uttered, "Make sure you all get all of that in his hand!"

"Indeed!" Entyce stated as her and Strawberry led him over in a corner and began dancing on him, right there with their street clothes still on.

I was still observing the large crowd and very large number of females that I had in attendance, when I looked to my right to see hot booty ass Lil' Kitty dancing on top of a table filled with some old ass men who all looked like they should've been in someone's nursing home. She spotted the look on my face as I shouted out to her, "Girl, you need to stop!"

She just looked back at me with that same unique smile on her face and said, "Forget you, Mike, their money is just as good as them broke ass young niggas' money!"

"Don't stop, girl. Forget what Mike is saying and get that paper!" was the voice I heard behind me.

I quickly turned around to see Peekachu with a smirk on her face. "Girl, if you don't get your crazy ass from behind me, yelling and shit, like you have lost your rabid ass mind!"

She looked all dejected as she recited, "Damn, Mike, that's how you treat a sister after your black ass leaves us with your whack ass cousin?"

"Yeah, Mike!" Suga Bear yelled as she stood right next to her close friend.

"Whatever. Get back to making that money!" I told them as I was walking away with Mignon, Tameia and Nicole still draped by my side.

But just as we were about to make a path for the dressing room, Tameia spotted two of her fans that played with the Jacksonville Jaguars. "Please, excuse me guys while I go make this money," she uttered as she hurried away with nothing but her lil' thick ass sashaying from side to side.

"Now, when did you all decide to make her a Murder Queen?" I asked Mignon as we continued walking, making our descent into the back of the club.

"Remind us to tell you after the club," Nicole spoke up, just as I spotted Tiger and her cousin Monique dancing over by the DJ booth on two big time dope boys from Jacksonville. They didn't see me due to the crowd of guys gathered around their table, watching the two of them doing girl on girl. Something that for some reason guys loved to see; while that really never turned me on.

When I finally got to the back of the club, the DJ spotted me and then gave me and the ladies on my arm our very own personal grand entrance introduction. "Give it up two times for that cool ass nigga who we all know as Michael Vallentino, the proud owner of half of the finest females inside the club tonight from Orlando, Florida. Who we all know as the muthafucking Florida Hot Girls!" Then he went to introduce the two females that were still by my side. "And three times for the two cute, lil' red thangs on his arm. One goes by the name of Mignon, with the other one calling herself Nicole!" The guys went wild at just the mention of their names. They both stood there hugging one another while smiling at all the attention they were getting.

Just as we had made it to the back of the club, I spotted my cousin Richard standing over to the left of the dressing room, telling one of the girls to have all the girls on the floor making money to dress back in.

"Nah, what's up, lil' cousin? Don't tell me that you are trying to be a boss now?" I asked him as I reached out to embrace him. This was the first time that I had seen him since the night at my place, when I actually thought about erasing him.

"Naw, big cuz. I saw your cool ass come through the door and I knew that if you caught any of the girls not dancing you would fine them right there on the spot," he said with a beer in one hand as he held tightly to a fat ass blunt in his other hand.

"You better believe it!" I replied, while marveling over the girls that Mignon had with her and how many Richard had with him. Richard had like nine with him while Mignon had twelve with her. I then informally leaned into Richard as the DJ continued mixing up the songs on the turntable, making sure that the club was hyped up with Trina saying that she was *Single Again*. In awe, I couldn't help but say to him, "Damn, my boy, the Florida Hot Girls are really representing up in this bitch tonight?"

His country ass looked back at me, half drunk. "Ain't they doe? That's how we do things around here, cousin. By the way, how was Puerto Rico?"

We both had wide smiles on our faces as I looked back over at him and said, "Puerto Rico was nice; a lil' different from the States. It's a place where you have to get used to as soon as you get there. The Estate where Rhynyia and her family resides in makes my house look like a small ass apartment with how huge it was."

"You serious?" he asked with a skeptical glare about his face.

"Yes, my young brother. When do I ever lie?"

"Man, I wish that I could have went over there with you and your laid back ass brother," he spoke as his head began to search the club for my brother. When he didn't see him, he came back at me with, "Where is he at anyway?" with his eyes still roaming.

"He's on his way back to Madison. Claims that he's about to start his own business and shit."

"Whatever, Mike. Man, stop playing," he said with a smile.

"No joke, my young-minded cousin," I replied as I turned my head, now looking out over the crowd and my ladies.

"You don't say. What kind of business is he about to start?"

I looked back over at him. "He said something along the line of pharmaceuticals."

This is when he took his blunt out of his crusted ass lips and tried to repeat the word, *pharmaceuticals*. "He's doing what?" he asked, now looking puzzled.

"Nothing, Richard. The club is so crunk up in here that it has me wanting to smoke on something nice and mellow," I uttered to him while laughing at my comment.

"You serious? You actually want something to smoke on?"

"Hell nah!" I replied as he pulled out a big ass bag of brown-looking weed that looked like some old grass that he had just been pulled out of someone's yard on the way to the club.

"Damn, cuz, you actually had me there for a minute!" he stuttered, a weed bag still in his hand.

"Yep. Now you know damn well that I don't smoke," I recited as I turned my head to witness the prettiest lil' thang walk from around the corner of the club.

"Hey, Mike." Her cute lips parted and said, "I'm so glad that you're finally back home." The radiant looking red young lady placed her arms around my neck and then placed a nice, wet, succulent kiss on my lips, causing my manhood to stiffen.

"Hello to you also, Ms. Bad ass Mo Money! What do you have on?" I asked her as she slowly turned around for me to witness sheer poetry in motion.

"Oh, do you like it? It's just a lil' something that I picked up earlier today at the mall," she said to me as she continued to do a full turn around so that I could see how nice her lil' plump ass looked in her attire.

After I picked my mouth up off of the floor, I spat, "It looks real nice on you, Mo Money. Make sure that when we leave, your ass is sitting in the front seat of that black Denali that's parked outside."

"You betta believe it, Mister Michael!" she replied as she walked away smiling.

But just as she was about to walk away, Nicole stepped in, catching her by her arm, then whispering into her ear, "Make sure there's enough room for me, too. We both are going to put it on his black ass tonight!"

Mo Money then reached out and placed a nice wet kiss on the lips of Nicole. Just as their lips unlocked, Mo Money said to her in her seductive ass voice, "I wouldn't have it any other way, my love." My early morning looked mighty fine from where I was standing.

Chapter 10
My Bad!

Richard's head was still gazing at the sight of Mo Money's nice ass walking away when, without even looking at me, he uttered, "Damn, cousin, she's fine as hell! Where did you find her fine ass at?" The poor man was star-struck as he dropped his blunt on the floor, due to him being mesmerized at the gorgeous female from the back.

Quickly thinking on my feet, I simply replied, "You know, for some strange reason, I can't seem to remember." I had to lie, due to me meeting her at Do-Dirty's funeral and I didn't want to bring that subject into our conversation.

Moments later, the DJ came back over the loud system. "Alright, ladies and gentleman, the club will be closing in another thirty minutes, so make sure you make these last few tips count!"

I was just getting into the groove of things when he made the announcement, with Richard still standing beside me bobbin' his head as the beat of the music resonated throughout the club. "Oh, by the way. Firstborn told me to tell you that you can have ole Strawberry."

He burst into laughter at my comment. "Man, fuck that! Ole girl seems to be with everybody!"

"I know that's right," I uttered, side smirk on my face as well. Needless to say, his ass was still bobbing to the beat, with me standing still, not moving my head at all. All due to me being at the point where I didn't even bob my head in the club whenever my ladies were making their money. Reason being is that I never wanted to lose sight of what I was there for, which was making money; not allowing the money to make me. While observing my ladies make their last few tips, JK walked by me with her fat ass hanging from her two-piece outfit. I playfully reached out and grabbed her by her arm. "Oh, so you're just going to walk your fine, thick ass right past me without speaking?"

She snapped her head around quickly. "Whatever, Mike. Your black ass saw me too, so you could have spoken to me first."

I paused for a brief moment, then gazed over her fine body before saying, "Yeah, you're absolutely right, JK. My bad. Hello and how in the hell are you?"

"I'm fine, Mike, and I'm glad that you're finally back home. Now, can I please have my arm back?" she said to me as I stumbled backwards.

"Oh, my bad."

"Whatever, boy. Now where are we all going for breakfast?"

"First of all, thank you, and if you're so glad that I'm back, why don't you give me a welcome home gift?" I asked her, gazing down at how her kitty cat was protruding out of her outfit.

This is when she cut a half smile at me. "Yeah, right, Mike. What would you want for your gift? And don't say my nice, fat ass kitty cat. Seems like you have enough of that. With Mo Money and any other one of these naïve, lil' fast ass females that seem to have your name in their mouths, every time they open it."

"Damn, it's like that?"

"Boy, please. You know how these lil' young chicks be foaming for your tall, black ass. You alright and shit, but if you were my man, I would have been killed your whorish ass by now!"

I swiftly dropped her arm back by her side. "Oh shit, well damn. I'm so sorry. I don't want no damn gift from your mean

43

ass. Just pay your tip out fee and we're good," I spat as Richard and myself laughed.

"You still didn't answer my question, Mike."

"My fault, what was that again?"

"Where are we eating breakfast at?"

"We' re going to eat at the Denny's off of Baymeadows, right next to the hotel."

She had a strange look on her face, then said, "You do know that we are all staying at the Red Roof Inn?"

"Why?"

"I have no idea. All I heard was that somebody had paid for our rooms. That's the only reason why we're up here this weekend."

"Okay, thanks. Do me a favor. Tell Nicole to come here for a minute, please?"

"Yep, see you." She hurried away, leaving me with the question as to why and who had paid for their rooms. I should have asked silly ass Richard, but just as she had said that, his ass slipped off.

Now during all of the mayhem, it never dawned on my black ass to ask Nicole and her crew why in the hell were the ladies at a warehouse tied up, about to be raped and murdered.

I was still standing there deep in thought, when Nicole walked up next to me. "Yeah, what's up, Mike?"

"Nicole," I said to her as I placed my hand on her arm, then walked her away. "Please tell me, why in the hell did some guys pay for the rooms this weekend?"

She looked back at me, then said, "I was going to tell you everything when we arrived back at the hotel."

"Why? Don't you think that I should know now?"

"Not really, Mike, and we should stop talking about it right here before we make a scene."

That's when I took my eyes off of her, to look around the club to see all the eyes that were on us, then back at her. "You're right, we'll talk later."

"Thanks, Mike," she said as she walked away, with me finding Richard, then walking over to him.

"Hey, Rich, don't let any of those girls go out that damn door until I get back!"

"Alright, cuz. I'll be right here smoking on these trees," he said to me while wetting his dry ass lips, getting ready to smoke some bap ass weed. "Hey, where are you headed anyway?" he shouted.

"Going to pay the girls' bar fee with Malik," I shouted back as I walked towards Malik's office.

On the way to his office, Mignon emerged out of nowhere, pulling me by my arm, then asking me, "Are you good or do you need one of us to go with you?"

Her mere beauty had me fucked up as I replied, "You're gonna make me make love to you, if it's the last thing I do, beautiful."

"Whatever, Mike. You wouldn't know what to do with all of this good ass pussy that's sitting off between my nice ass thighs!" she replied as she grinned at me.

"Damn, Mignon, you just don't know how fucking bad I want you!" I said as my heart beat rapidly.

"Believe me, I already know. But I will never cross my sisters all because of you. Now, do you need me to accompany you back there or are you good?"

I then stole a kiss from her and said, "Stay here and watch the girls and my back. And by the way, you have some soft ass lips!"

She looked directly in my eyes and said, "If you think that those lips are soft, you should see how my lips that don't smile feel up against a long, hard, big, black dick!"

I just stood there stuck, watching her walk away in her tight, nice black, fitted Baby Phat jeans.

Chapter 11
Missing In Action!

As soon as I went to turn around to venture off into Malik's office, I bumped into Tarshay, who was strolling out of one of the VIP rooms, head held down.

She was shocked to see that I was the one who she had bumped into as she looked up into my face and said, "Oh. Excuse me, Mike. When did you get back in town?"

"About a few hours ago, young lady."

"Welcome home," she said with open arms.

"Thank you. I see that you're still making your money the easy way."

"Yes, that I am. I see that you finally brought your black ass back home to mama."

"Whatever, Tarshay. I missed you guys, so I had to get back here soon as possible. Just to make sure that all you ladies made that money."

She was lazily trying to fix her attire when she recited, "You know, I have really missed you and what was his name again?" Her face had a half smile on it.

"Who?" I asked as she pointed down at my manhood. "Oh him. His name is John Boy." We laughed for a brief moment. "Whatever, girl. Take your hot ass on inside the dressing room and dress back in before your black ass gets left up here in Jacksonville."

She smirked, then turned her nose up at me. "Now, Mike, you know damn well that you can't leave all this up here in Jacksonville." She then pointed down at her fat pussy print that was protruding outside of her outfit. "But if you do, I've made enough money up here to buy you and me a brand-new car, so that the both of us can drive home in."

"Yeah, okay," I spoke while walking up to Malik's office door.

She continued yelling at my head. "You know where to find my fine ass when you get finished with him!" She then turned and walked towards the dressing room, as I knocked twice on Malik's door.

The door slightly opened up with him ushering me inside so that the commotion outside wouldn't drown out him hearing what the person on the other line was saying to him. I guess I had caught him right dab smack in the middle of an important phone call. He cut his eyes over at me. "Have a seat, Boss Man." Then, he turned his attention back to his phone call.

Just as I sat, I reached into my pants pocket, pulling out several crisp hundred-dollar bills, so that I could pay the girls' tip out fee.

His eyes told his lips to smile as I placed six hundred dollars into his hands. After counting it, he nodded in approval on the amount in which I gave him. I then eased my tired black ass onto his doodoo brown stained couch that he had adorned inside his office.

"Alright, I'll check on that, but like I said earlier, Tracey. I haven't heard or seen Punkin or Marquise all day," he spat as I sat there intensively listening to his conversation.

I mumbled to myself, "Damn, he knew them busta ass niggas, too?"

"Yeah, as soon as I hear anything, I'll let you know, I promise. If they are in trouble, we will find the people that they have a problem with and deal with it from there. Peace." He then hung up. "Now, what's good with you, Mike?" He asked as he faced me.

"I'm good, my nigga. What's up with you though?" I asked as he sat down, now rubbing his head with his right hand.

He then slid open his desk where he pulled out a thick bag of what looked like Kush weed. "Nothing much, just a lot of bullshit, that's all. You want to hit some of this shit, my man?" he asked me with a side smirk covering up his devilish looking face.

"Nah, partner, I'm good."

"Suit yourself. That just means there's more for me." He then licked the long blunt and put fire to the end of it. The brother had lungs like a fucking vacuum cleaner as he took a long pull, then blew out billows of smoke over his head. "Well, at least somebody is doing good round this bitch. How 'bout my baby sister just called me crying about her punk ass baby daddy, Punkin, being missing in action all day."

I looked at the young brother with a quizzical look on my face as. "What?" I was trying to sound like I gave a flying fuck about the dead nigga.

"Yeah, man. Hell, how am I supposed to know what the lil' nigga has going on?" he said as he continued pulling slowly on the nice smelling weed.

Don't get me wrong. At that juncture of my life I didn't smoke, and couldn't understand why most people did smoke weed. But if I did, I sure would have smoked on that Kush his black ass was smoking on that morning.

"I hear you. Does she have any idea where he might be?" I asked as I thought hard about why he was with those bustas at that warehouse.

"Not a clue, homie. She probably thinks that his ass is somewhere tricking with one of your girls," he remarked.

"Nah, not one of my chicks," I quickly said. But right then is when I made a mental note to find out which one of my dumb ass girls had been fucking with the nigga.

"Oh, yeah? Well, wasn't it him and his boys who had took that one chick Strawberry out a few weeks ago?"

"I really don't know. You know I really don't ask the girls who they trick with." I replied, heart racing.

"Mike, stop it! Man, I seen what you and your cousin did with them niggas that night."

"Man, that was nothing."

"Whatever, Mike."

"I wonder what would make you or her think that he was out with one of my girls."

He looked serious for a brief moment. "I'm just kidding with you, Mike, man. Calm down."

We laughed.

"Yeah, you almost had me there with that one, playa."

"I know. I could tell by the way you jumped up in your seat. But on the real, I did see him all up in your girl, Lil' Kitty's ear last night," he uttered with a serious ass unit on his face.

"Oh yeah? Well, I can tell you he can't be with her because her funky ass is in the dressing room, getting dressed right now. And the last time I checked, there was no nigga named Punkin in there with her."

"C'mon, Mike, man. I'm just saying that I saw them two talking. Hell, I don't know where his ass is. Like I told her, I haven't seen the nigga all day."

All I could do as I sat there listening to that nigga, was ponder the question of why in the hell were my ladies even at that warehouse with Punkin and his homies. Now here I was answering questions about his disappearance. I knew I had a problem, and I knew exactly where Punkin's lil' narrow ass was. So as Malik sat there slow fucking his blunt, I abruptly stood to my feet and recited, while yawning and stretching my arms, "I hear you. Well, a young brother like myself is kind of tired from my flight, so if things are straight with us, my ladies and I are going to head on back to the hotel so I can get some sleep."

He stood up too, preventing me from reaching for the doorknob. "Nonsense, lil' homie. You and some of your girls just got here."

This is when I had to put on one of my best performances ever. "Yeah, we did. But the DJ just said about forty minutes ago that this fine establishment that you have here was about to close." We both stood there staring at each other with me feeling a slight bit awkward.

"Mike, this is my fine establishment here and we close when I say we close!" His face held a sinister grin as he slid his chair up under him and sat back down.

"I hear you, but I just flew back in from Puerto Rico, that flight has me tired as hell."

"So, you all flew straight here to Jacksonville from Puerto Rico?" he asked, eyes about to bulge out of his black ass face.

"Indeed. I really missed all of my girls, so I had the pilot fly us straight here."

He started smiling as he looked up at me and said, "I hear you, kid. Hey. I know what I wanted to ask you," he said as he placed what was left of his blunt down on the table.

"What's that, playa?"

"Man, what is up with the one lil' honey on your team that they call Mo Money?"

I started smiling just as soon as I heard her name. "Oh, that lil' shortie. She is fine, isn't she?" I asked, now feeling myself.

"Yes, she is, that's why I'm asking you about her." He just knew that he was going to take her home. He had already been with a few of the girls and always felt as if he could have his pick of anyone of them that he wanted. Like the time he took Chanel and Lil' Kitty home after the club one night. Well, his black ass was supposed to be with Chanel, but I would find out later that when she fell asleep, Lil' Kitty found her way to his bed and fucked him. When Chanel got up the next morning and found Lil' Kitty laying next to him naked, she put them paws on her lil' narrow ass. Let's just say after that night, Lil' Kitty made sure she picked the right dude to fuck.

"So, what's up, Mike? Hook me up with the lil' baddie," he pleaded, half smirk on his face.

I stared the brother down for a brief moment, then said, "Hell, all I can tell you is that the lil' shortie is something special once you get her fine ass in the bedroom."

His half smirk now turned into a full out shit-eating ass smile. "That's all I need to know, homie. Man, hook me up with her fine lil' short ass!" he growled as he rubbed his two hands together. The brother almost looked like he was a crackhead with the way he was barking and pleading.

"I would love to, Malik, but I think she's already taken, big homie," I uttered as I turned to place my hand on the doorknob of his small office.

But just as I opened the door, guess who came barging inside with a wide, beaming smile plastered all over her gorgeous face?

Chapter 12
New Found Friend!

Her smile and grace jolted me at the door. "Here you are! Mignon told me that I could find you in here." She then turned to Malik still smiling as she said, "Hey, Malik." She stood in the doorway, looking flawless, with some tight black shorts on, with her white cut-off Florida Hot Girl T-Shirt. Her nice sized breast could barely hide through the cut-off shirt that sat right above her belly button.

Malik, one who is never short for words swiftly said, "What's good, Mo Money? Mike and myself were just talking about you."

She then put her hands on her waist as she kissed me on my cheek, then turned to look him directly in his cold black eyes. "Oh, for real? What were y'all saying about little ole me?"

This is when he tried to cut a half smile at her. "I was just asking him to hook me up with you." He spoke with confidence and assurance. I guess since he had his way with simple minded ass Lil' Kitty and some of the others, he felt like he had a chance. Wrong!

Because just as his thin ass lips parted, she came back at him quickly with, "Oh yeah? Well, he didn't tell you that all of this was already taken?" She turned around to allow his eyes to take in such a beautiful sight, then placing her arms around me, pulling me closer to her body.

"He was trying to, but we didn't get that far into the conversation."

I was just standing there looking at how nice her fat ass looked and imaging how nice it would look from the back with my hands on her soft ass cheeks as I slid my manhood off into her tight womb. The place that I would put two twin daughters inside of one day, way down the road. Need I say that the only time Mo Money ever turned her back on me was when I was hitting her from behind.

I then snapped back to reality as I asked her, "So you're 'bout ready to go get something to eat?"

"Yes, boo," she answered as she kissed me on the lips. Looking back over at Malik, she said, "All of this belongs to Michael."

The bother just stood there smiling at the both of us as we walked out of his office, hand in hand. "You are a bad ass nigga, Mike," he shouted as we stepped out of his office.

"Yeah, that's what they say. We'll see you next week, kid. Take it easy," I replied as we both hurried ourselves up out of there and around the bar.

"'Bout fucking time, Mike. We thought that you and black ass Malik were in there fucking the shit out of ole Mo Money! As long as it took you all to come from his office!"

"Damn, Suga Bear, that's how you feel?"

"Yeah, Mike. We're all out here in these trucks, ready to grab something to eat. Then get to our rooms so that we can get some sleep."

"My bad." I replied.

"Don't worry about her, baby, she's just mad that I made all the money tonight," Mo Money said into my ear.

"I see," I said to her as we walked outside where everyone was all ready to go grab something to eat.

"Hey, Mike, where are we going to eat at?" Richard yelled out to me, still somewhat high.

"The Denny's off of Baymeadows Plaza. And make sure you have all of your girls' tip out fee for me when we get there!"

"Alright, I'm right behind you, cousin!" he yelled as I jumped in the driver's seat of my truck while Mignon and her crew got inside the vehicle with her. Mo Money did just as she was told and sat her lil' red ass in the front seat of my vehicle, right along with her newfound friend.

I was shocked and surprised just as well as the rest of the girls were when Nicole decided to sit up front, right beside Mo Money. "Oh, what a surprise to see you, Ms. Nicole," I uttered as she sat there smiling at the both of us.

"Don't be. What was I supposed to do? Let Mo Money here have all the fun this morning?" she jokingly asked while looking over at me with a devious smile, letting me know that she was down with whatever after breakfast.

"Nah, not at all my dear." I replied as I looked at both of them sitting there talking amongst one another. "Okay, well I guess we're off to grab something to eat."

"Yes, we are. Now hurry up, because we're all starving!" Mo Money spat just as I had pulled onto the interstate, headed towards Baymeadows.

My head was in the clouds as I sped down the highway with my two favorite girls in the group seated right beside me, when an odd voice from the rear of my truck yelled out, "Don't get that hot lil' ass too comfortable sitting up there in the front seat, Mo Money!" Suga Bear spat with a slight bit of sarcasm in her voice.

"And why is that, little Ms. Suga Bear?" Mo Money asked as she snapped her head around, causing her sharp eyes to stare at her dancing partner.

Suga Bear cleared her parched throat and then came back with, "Because, after two weeks of sitting up there, he replaces the old chick with a new chick, that's why! So, like I said, don't get too comfortable up there in the front seat! And my damn name ain't no damn Suga Bear, hoe."

"Alright, Step, watch your mouth," I chimed in as I stared at her from my rear-view mirror.

"Whatever, Mike, she started it first."

"What the hell ever Suga Bear, you started it off by telling me that bullshit about some new bitch taking my fucking place up front, so bitch I had to come back at that ass!" Mo Money yelled as the tension in the truck went up another level.

"I got your bitch just as soon as Mike stops this fucking truck! I'm gonna get so deep off into that red ass of yours!" Step—I mean Suga Bear— shouted as she paused from counting up her money.

"Nah-nah-nah, we're not having any of that shit this morning. Not on my fucking watch! So, just chill the fuck out, Step!" Nicole blurted out as she turned to stare back at Step, seated in the back of the truck between Peekachu and her sister Chazz, who wouldn't have been any help to her sister if something did jump off, all due to her being high as a kite already.

"Ump, I guess you hoes heard that shit. Now, why don't y'all just chill out and continue counting up your money," JK said as she sat behind me smiling.

"Nah, let that ass get smart, so Suga Bear can beat the brakes off of her ass!" Lil' Kitty barked as she sat there, looking forward to seeing the fight.

"Shut the hell up, Lil' Kitty! We ain't having that between the members of this group!" I said to her while trying to calm the girls down.

"Why are you so certain that Suga Bear will be the one beating the brakes off of someone? Last time anyone got the brakes beat off of their ass was when Chyna put them paws on your lil' thin ass!" Nicole said as she smirked.

"Whatever. I was getting with her ass just as well as she got with me," Lil' Kitty replied as she sat there smiling while cutting her eyes over in Chyna's direction. Making sure she knew exactly where her adversary was seated.

"Alright, enough already, ladies. Please calm the fuck down. Hell, I just got back in town and y'all already at each other's throats."

"I'm just saying, Mike, you might as well tell her the truth. Because right after them two weeks are up, your slick ass is going to put a new female up there in that front seat!" Step continued as she leaned forward, trying to get her point across.

"Step, Suga Bear. Whatever it is. Your ass doesn't have to worry about this front seat, just as long as you have a seat," I yelled while trying to calm her emotions down.

Then out of nowhere, Lil' Kitty jumped back in yelling, "Yeah, Mike, you might as well tell your lil' boo thang up there, that in two weeks, there's going to be a new girl you bring to this group and you're going to be fucking her just like you did the rest of us girls! So that will be her seat for the next few weeks, until you find another one to replace her with."

"Damn, Lil' Kitty, if I didn't know any better, it sounds like your lil' hot ass has already been up there in the front seat!"

"She has!" Chyna burst out with as the entire truck of ladies burst into laughter.

Chapter 13
Pure Meat!

After the laughter died down a shy, innocent voice yelled out. "Ah, hell nah, he hasn't fucked me yet!"

All heads turned to her as Nicole recited, "Oh, so you're saying that you want him to fuck you as well, huh?"

"Nah, that's not what I meant to say. My bad. I'm so sorry," the slim white female friend of Charlie B said as her face turned beet red with embarrassment.

"Excuse me, ladies," Lil' Kitty interrupted, just as the noise level had went back down. "Nah, Mo Money. You see one thing about Mike is that if he has fucked you, it only means one thing."

"And what's that, Lil' Kitty?" Mo Money asked as she turned around again with her face still holding a slight smile.

"Hell, you can answer that for yourself, young lady. Aren't you sitting in the front seat?" JK asked as she placed her money back inside of her bag.

"Yes," Mo Money answered, still holding onto her cute smile.

"Well then, I guess that he must really like you, so you have nothing to worry about."

Mo Money felt a bit of assurance as she turned back around, looking over at me and Nicole, still smiling. We all thought that the conversation was over, until her familiar voice came back with, "But don't smile too long, Ms. Lady, because just as sure as that nigga has two legs and that beautiful smile of his, there will be another chick sitting in that front seat in the next two weeks, smiling just like your country ass is doing right now!"

"And why is that, Lil' Kitty?" Mo Money asked.

"Because every day is a new day for him to go out and recruit new females, who ultimately join this growing group and become a Florida Hot Girl."

"Now her ass is right about that one," JK recited as she stared out of the window.

"Yes, that she is. But it seems like her lil' narrow ass has been up here in the front seat just as well as I am," Nicole barked, sounding a tad bit angry.

"Nah, never that!" Lil' Kitty yelped, trying to sound convincing, with only her and I knowing of the many nights after a long, tiring show that she had her legs propped up over the back seat of my vehicle, while I plunged in and out of her fine ass, with ten and a half inches of pure meat, engulfed inside of her tight pussy. I would have to be the first one to say, one thing about that Lil' Kitty, was that she always had some good pussy.

As I continued speeding down interstate 95, headed towards Denny's, my head started spinning, pondering if my thirsty ass brother made it out of the airport with all of that Yayo. Then my head began to throb even more while thinking of my precious Rhynyia and her sister, wondering if they made it in the air safely. With those mere thoughts clouding my already confused mind, reality started to sink in while looking over at Nicole. Still wanting to know why in the hell were the Murder Queens even at that abandoned warehouse about to get raped then murdered?

Not only was I now involved in another hideous crime, but what type of effect would take over the families of those dead individuals that we had left behind? Not only were their families about to receive the worst news that a person would want to hear, it was the simple fact of me living with the face of those guys in my head for the rest of my natural born life. Not only was I apart of their devious minded deed, but I knew who the girls were who took them out. The only comfort that I could receive from their actions that took place was the mere fact that if they hadn't done what they had to do, they would be the ones inside of that warehouse with a bullet hole in their heads. Something that I knew I wouldn't want to bear. So, as I tried to process all of that through my thick ass skull, I heard the Weezy Jefferson sounding voice of Chanel.

"So, Mike, what time are we checking out of the hotel in the morning?"

"Round about twelve, Chanel," I replied as I turned on my blinker, signaling that I was about to exit the highway.

"Okay, thank you," she replied in her deep, raspy voice that just drove me fucking crazy every time she opened her damn mouth. If she hadn't been so damn fine, there was no way in hell I would have let her continue to be in the group.

Once all three of the vehicles pulled up to Denny's, everyone jumped out, all exhausted and ready to consume a very much needed breakfast. Including me. Or at least I was until I heard Entyce yell for me from the rear of my truck. "Excuse me, Mike, can I speak with you for a minute, please?"

"You guys go on in. I'll be inside in a few." Mo Money and Nicole stood next to me, looking like they couldn't breathe without me next to them.

"Bae, do you want me to order you what you usually have for breakfast?" Nicole asked while Mo Money held her arm as if they were a couple, ready for wifey material.

"Yes, baby girl, go ahead." I replied with my devilish smile across my face.

The elegant lady of the night had her head down as I slowly approached her. I kind of knew what was about to happen as I eased up closer to her. I just didn't want it to be happening at that very moment in time.

"Yeah, what's on your mind, young lady?"

She looked up at me with her cute brown eyes. "Mike, I just can't do this shit anymore."

I placed my arm around her, trying my best to console her, simply because I knew what she was going through. "I understand, Entyce. I don't blame you. When my sister and you ladies told me about the Murder Queens, I tried to tell y'all then, that this wasn't something that I wanted for you ladies. But no, you guys insisted on being the Murder Queens."

She was staring me straight in the eyes, with hot tears slowly crawling down her lovely face and replied ever so softly, "You're right, Mike, and believe me when I tell you that I would still want to be a Murder Queen and a Florida Hot Girl. But when that guy pulled out that gun and pointed it at my head, then stripped me naked. Made something inside my head snap, which caused me to realize that life was too short to end up dying like that."

I shook my head, feeling her pain as she spoke. "I do understand that this shit is some real serious business."

"Yes, it is!" she uttered as she wiped her face, then spat, "And besides, Mike, I'm pregnant."

I sat down on the rear bumper of my truck and took a deep breath, then stared back at her and thought real hard before saying, "Damn, Entyce, so y'all having a lil' baby, huh?"

She began to cry even harder as I sat there looking into her eyes.

"Hey, why are you still crying? You should be the happiest girl in the world with news like that," I said, sounding so concerned about her and her unborn child, while her face had snot and tears uncontrollably racing down her cheeks.

She angrily began to wipe them away as I handed her one of my silk handkerchiefs so that she could properly wipe her nose and face. Just as she had wiped away all the mucous and tears, she said something that threw my black ass for a loop. Something that I couldn't believe. But that's what I was supposed to get, for allowing a snake into my den. "Because the baby's father is a fucking rat!"

"What?" I shouted as I quickly jumped up.

"A fucking rat bitch ass nigga! When you left for Puerto Rico, I had to put his nosey, ungrateful ass out! Only to find out later that the lil' ass nigga went to the cops and we believe that he might have said something to them about our extra night time activities."

I was still trying to focus on what I had just heard as she kept calling out my name.

"Mike, Mike, say something."

I fell back down hard onto the bumper, then looked up at her, asking her, "What do you want me to say, Entyce? Reese can put us all behind bars for a very long time. So damn long that we might not never see daylight again." She just stood there, looking lost, then trying to hand me back what she had just blew her nose with. I looked at it, then stared back at her, before uttering. "Ahh, hell nah, you can keep that shit."

She coyly smiled at me, trying not to laugh, then said, "I'm really going to miss your good humor and crazy ass jokes."

"Yeah, hell, I'm going to miss it too if that short ass nigga of yours rats us all out."

"No worries, Mike, you can bet your house on this. The last person that I have to kill before I leave this group will be the rat who got me pregnant."

"I sure hope so. There's no telling what he might have already told them damn people," I said to her as we both turned to walk inside with the rest of the group.

"I already know. But I got you and this group of women that I'm surely going to miss, Mike."

My face held a slight smile as I looked down at her and said, "I know you are and we're going to miss you too, Entyce. Now, let's eat. I'm hungry as a muthafucker!"

We both walked inside to see all of the ladies over to the right of the establishment waiting on us to join them. Nicole and Mo Money had acquired a nice booth off to the side as Mo Money yelled out to me. "Mike, over here!"

"Girl, he sees your lil' red ass. Just chill!"

"Whatever, Lil' Kitty. You always running that mouth of yours!" Mo Money said with a mean smirk across her face. "Listen, lil' girl. You don't want none of this over here. So if I was you, I would just shut your damn mouth!" Mo Money tediously eased up in her seat, peering over at Lil' Kitty.

"Whatever, bitch. You just mad cause your lil' DJ friend had his eyes on me all night and throwing me his entire paycheck for the night whenever your lil' thirsty ass left him alone!" Lil' Kitty tried to jump up from the table, but quickly sat back down when she saw the angry face that Nicole held.

"Alright, Lil' Kitty, don't get shit twisted up in here. I'll have your short ass on the next bus back to Orlando if you even think about touching her! Now sit that hot ass down and order something to eat!"

"Damn, where did her fiery ass come from?" Chyna asked as she sat there smiling at all the commotion between the two feisty young ladies.

"Not now, Chyna. You two calm down. We're supposed to be family, so just chill."

"Whatever, Mike. She started it," Mo Money said as she went back to counting up her money.

"Nah, Mike, it's just that your lil' chick here thinks that she is the shit since she's fucking you!"

"What? You jealous, Lil' Kitty?" Mo Money snapped back.

"Lil' Kitty, please. She doesn't feel like that. You ladies who keep fucking with her are the ones who feel like that," Nicole said as she stood up for Mo Money's defense.

"I tell you what. The next female that says something to her in the wrong way has a fifty dollar fine. I mean that shit! Now please, can everyone order something to eat so we can get the hell out of here!" I said in a very loud tone that caused the other people eating to stop and stare at what I had going on. Once I seen that all eyes were on me, I had to swiftly speak. "Sorry, everyone, please excuse us over here."

"Damn, I didn't know that we had all eyes on us."

"Yes, Mo Money. When you get loud that's what usually happens," Nicole said as she smiled at her, then looking up at me, placing her tired head on my shoulder. "I hear you. Oh, I ordered you the usual. Steak and over easy eggs with raisin toast."

"Did you order me the hash browns with everything inside of them?"

"Yes, Mike," Nicole said as she smirked.

"Okay, just making sure. Now can we talk in front of Mo Money?"

"Yes, Mike. She's almost one of us, now."

"Cool, now someone please tell me why in the hell were you guys at that warehouse?"

Chapter 14
What Did I Do?

Mo Money's mouth fell wide open as Nicole stared me directly in the eyes. "Like I told you earlier, Mike, it's a long story." She sat straight up in her seat and sighed.

"Well, I guess you better start talking then." I picked up my glass of orange juice and dully sipped.

"Don't you want to wait until you finish your breakfast?" she asked, trying to hold back her guilt.

"Nah, not really. I need to know why you and them damn Murder Queens were in danger."

"Well, maybe I should let our fearless leader Mignon speak on that one. She's the one who put the flawless plan in effect."

I sighed to myself as I became agitated with Nicole and how she was beating around the bush. "It's whatever. All I want to know is what caused you guys to be in the thick of all this danger. And to think, if those thugs would have taken you girls out, no telling what they would have done to the rest of the Florida Hot Girls."

"I know," she said as she drowsily sipped on a hot cup of coffee.

"I don't think so, Nicole, so start talking. After that I want to know how you guys convinced lil' ass Mo Money here to join the group," I replied as I laid back inside the booth.

"Oh, I can answer that one for you, Mike," Mo Money excitedly said in a light outburst.

Nicole's head twisted at the sound of her voice, then turning back to me she said, "Okay, Mike, it all started when…" By the time she had finished telling me what had caused them to be in Jacksonville, tied and gagged, about to be raped and killed, I was through with my breakfast.

I had just dropped my fork back down on my plate, when Mo Money blurted out. "Damn, this is some real, serious shit we're into."

I looked over at her and then back at Nicole before I said, "So, you sure that this is something that you want to start doing?"

"Hell yeah, without a doubt. I can't wait!" She held a smile as she sat there eager to make her first kill.

"For real?"

"Indeed. I would have been with them tonight, but I had to fall back at Nicole's directions of course." She innocently smiled at me.

I looked over at Nicole and said, "I see. So they got to you guys through Lil' Kitty's ass I presume?" I asked this question as I cut my eyes over at her, sitting there at the table, still stuffing her mouth full of the pancakes that she was trying to finish.

"Yes. Matter of fact, those guys wanted us up here so fucking bad, that they actually paid for the rooms."

"Damn!"

"Yep, and the only way that they could have got to her was through the heifers cell phone number that she keeps giving out." Nicole stared at Lil' Kitty.

"I know, that's why I tell you ladies to never give out your damn phone number, whenever we're out of town."

Lil' Kitty looked up to see us staring at her. She smiled at me before she asked. "What? Why are your eyes over here, Mister? Shouldn't you be looking at them?" She pointed her fork in the ladies' direction.

"Not now, Lil' Kitty. When your ass gets through eating, you might want to check on when the next Greyhound bus pulls up out of Jacksonville, headed for Orlando."

Her fork dropped hard, just as well as her face. Then as if she commanded them, hot tears began to well up in the bottom of her precious eyes. "Why, what did I do?"

***

Four Hours Prior
Jacksonville International

The private plane of Pierre Santiago had just taken off. Rhynyia and her sister were relaxing when Maria ran back to the passenger area. "Princess, we have a problem!"

Rhynyia had just closed her eyes when she opened the right one and said, "What is it now?"

"It seems as though the police have a helicopter on our tail as we speak."

"Oh shit! They must have realized who this plane belongs to!" she shouted as she jumped up. "Move, I have to get to the cockpit!" she shouted as she pushed Maria to the side and made her way down the aisle, headed directly for the cockpit. Just as she got to the door, she turned to Maria and asked, "Was all of the cocaine taken off the plane?"

"To the best of my knowledge, Princess."

"We all better hope so. If not, we might be stuck over here inside of a jail cell for a mighty long time!" Rhynyia shouted as she opened the door of the cockpit. The plane had only been up in the air for about twenty minutes when Miguel spotted the helicopter behind them. "Miguel, where are we?"

"Right now, we are in a small portion of the Atlantic Ocean," he replied, sweat drifting down his face.

"How many helicopters are there behind us?"

"Right about now, it looks like one." He was frightened half to death.

"Okay, how do we know that it's the police?" she asked as she placed a pair of the headsets over her head.

"They have been telling me to turn around since we took off."

"I see." She sighed, then hesitated for a brief moment.

"What do we do, Princess?"

"Hold on for a moment. There's no way that we can land this bird back at the airport. For if they run the dogs through here, they just might sniff out what we had on board."

"I know. So, what do I do?" he asked, just as Maria and Natasha came up front with the worst news ever.

"Rhynyia, we have a big problem."

Rhynyia's head swiftly turned around, face stern. "What is it now, Natasha?"

"There seems to be more of the cocaine on the plane than we knew about."

"What? How much?" She asked in a panic.

"Ten more Kilos of pure uncut cocaine."

"Is it father's?"

"I can't tell until we get this bird down."

"Well, we won't be doing that," she said, then looked back over at Miguel. "We have to take this plane where no one would dare go."

His eyes showed signs of pure terror as he yelled, "No, Princess, there's no way that I will place us in that type of danger!"

"Right now, we don't have any other choice. Fly this son of a bitch over the Bermuda Triangle, now!"

Chapter 15
Beat It!

I didn't know if I was angry or furious, when I answered her. "Too much, now go ahead and make that call. And while you're at it, call the local cab company so they can give your ass a ride to the bus station downtown." I had just turned my head back to face the two sitting with me, when she jumped up screaming.

"So, what? You're mad at me because I said something to your little whore!"

The entire establishment got eerily silent as the word whore rolled off her lips. Over in the corner of the place, I could have sworn that I heard Suga Bear go, "Owwwwww! It's 'bout to be on now!"

Just as fast as she uttered those sentiments, Mo Money quickly jumped up with fire in her eyes, screaming, "See bitch, I told your lil' ass about starting with me!" The next thing we all seen was just about as entertaining as watching a Mike Tyson fight. Only difference was that this one was live and in action right before our very eyes.

Mo Money flew over the booth, swinging wildly in midair as her right fist caught Lil' Kitty flush against her left cheek.

Pancakes and everything else she had in her mouth flew everywhere when her mouth opened unexpectedly. Before Lil' Kitty even realized that she was hit, another punishing blow hit her smack dead in the stomach. I think it was a left uppercut that had her ass bent over now, then another blow to the back of her small head. This caused the poor girl to stumble over her own two feet, allowing Mo Money a clear right jab to the girl's right eye as she sluggishly turned around. Her poor eye didn't even see it coming, when another left jab closed that same eye. I swore that I heard her eye say, "Goodnight!" as it closed.

"Damn!" Richard shouted while placing his closed fist up over his open mouth.

"Oh shit, man that one chick is beating the shit out of that poor girl!" One of the paying customers shouted.

"Is there anyone at least going to help her?" Another customer shouted.

"Hell nah, the lil' trick has been asking for that ass whooping all weekend!" Pekachu shouted as she stood up right next to Chazz and Step, cheering Mo Money on.

After Lil' Kitty made an attempt to strike back and missed, I felt like she had had enough. "Mo Money, calm down!" I shouted, trying to get in between the two, when Lil' Kitty lunged at Mo Money. The girl was quick on her feet as she shifted to the side, then swinging back at Lil' Kitty, flying right past her. Since one of her eyes were closed, she swung awkwardly. Once Lil' Kitty had her back towards Mo Money, she punched the shit out of her back.

"Ahhh hell nah!" Lil' Kitty screamed in pain and anguish.

The next thing everyone heard was, "Fights Over!" Nicole yelled with a wicked smirk on her face.

"Oh shit, damn that lil' heifer can really go!" One of the girls shouted.

The manager of the restaurant shouted, "No-no-no! I'm calling the police!"

By then, I felt sorry for the way Mo Money had beat the shit out of Lil' Kitty and tried to stop it by stepping between them. That's when I caught a vicious right jab in the palm of my hand. I turned to Mo Money. "Enough already. The poor girl has already had enough. Nicole, grab her and calm her ass down," I said as I saw the anger and hate in Mo Money's red eyes.

When Nicole got over to her, she quickly had to say, "Hey, hey, it's over, calm down! You have proved your point." Nicole and Mignon drug her away from a badly battered and beaten Lil' Kitty who was trying her best to get to her feet.

"I'm cool, man, let me go! Now, bitch, say another word and the next time they won't be able to pull me off of that ass!" Mo Money yelled as they dragged her out of the door.

"Yeah, whatever, hoe!" Lil' Kitty barked as I tried to help her up.

I was glad that it was over and glad that Mo Money didn't hear her say the word hoe, again. "Alright, Lil' Kitty, there you go with that mouth of yours. Haven't you had enough already?"

"Alright, Lil' Kitty, that's what got that ass looking like that now. Girl, you better calm down," Chyna said as she and a few of the other females continued laughing at the way Lil' Kitty's hair was all over her head.

"Whatever. Where's my phone?" Lil' Kitty asked as she pulled away from me with anger.

I felt bad for her, so I let go of her and said, "Forget about it. You can ride back with us and no, you wasn't riding the bus because of her. It was all due to you passing your damn number out."

She sat back down, in the wrong seat of course.

"Listen up ladies, the punk ass Manager has called the police, so grab your things and head to the door. Hopefully I can straighten things out with him."

"You don't have to tell me twice. I have a warrant too, so I'm gone!" Chazz uttered as she placed a twenty-dollar bill on the table and ran for the door.

I had three warrants myself, so there was no way in hell I wanted to stay there and deal with the Po-Pos. "Hey, y'all go ahead. I'll pay for this!" I said as the ladles still were baffled at what they had just witnessed.

Suga Bear looked up at me while trying to grab her sister's money back off of the table. "For real, Mike, you're paying for everyone's breakfast?"

"Hell nah, I'll just collect the money when I pick up my tip out fee! Now get out of here, Suga Bear!'"

"Fuck you, Mike. I told your black ass about that Suga Bear shit!"

I quickly looked back at her and said, "Girl, pretend that ass is Michael Jackson and just beat it!" Moments later, I had slid the manager two crisp c-notes and he told me that he would just tell the police that the incident had been contained. "Thank you, sir," I said to the man as Tameia and a few of the girls were walking outside with me to our vehicles. Now standing there amongst the entire squad, I got the chance to say, "Okay, check out time is around eleven this morning. It's like six right now, which means that we only have a few hours before we have to get right back up. Get some sleep and don't be late or you'll be living here in Jacksonville for a few days."

"Whatever, Mike. Like I told your black ass earlier, I have enough money to buy you and me a car so that we can drive back home."

"Damn, Tarshay, you balling like that?"

"Yes, girl," she said as she cut a quick smile over at me.

"Damn, what nigga were you dancing on, chick?" Peekachu asked, still laughing at what she had just witnessed.

"That same one that Lil' Kitty danced on earlier and told me that he had some money that he wanted to spend on me inside the VIP room."

"I know that's right!" JK said as she stepped back inside of my truck.

"So, you made the money that Lil' Kitty was supposed to have made?" Suga Bear insinuated, trying to start up more confusion.

"Yep."

"Whatever. Y'all hoes— I mean girls— are just jealous," Lil' Kitty remarked as she lethargically sat inside of Richard's truck, feeling the aftereffects of her *title defense*.

The air was instantly filled with laughter as I heard Peekachu shout, "Some hoes never learn!"

Then it was as if another awful chapter was about to unfold right before our very eyes. For some odd reason, I turned to see our waitress, standing outside crying and talking with her manager. I could barely hear her as I think that she had said something about an emergency that she had to attend to.

The poor child walked right past us when Mignon asked her, "Is everything okay?"

The young lady stopped for just a brief moment as I caught a glimpse at her name tag, then thought to myself. *Damn, I heard that name somewhere before, about a few hours ago.* "No, not really. My mother just called me and told me that they found my baby daddy shot to death at some warehouse with a few of his homies!"

"Damn," I mumbled to myself.

Mignon placed her arms around the young lady, trying to console her. "I'm so sorry to hear that, sweetheart." Mignon tried her best to conceal her knowledge of what they had just did.

"Thank you." The young lady uttered as she grayly stepped inside of the off red colored Nissan Altima, waiting for her in the parking lot.

They had just sped out of the parking lot when the Murder Queens gathered around me, looking somewhat startled and concerned. "You guys have any idea who that was?" I asked them as I turned my lips to the side in somewhat of an unbelievable smirk on my face.

Mignon was the first person to answer. "Yeah, one of them guys' baby mama, right?"

"Yeah, that was the lil' nigga with the play dick shoved up his ass, I think."

"His name was Punkin," Strawberry stated as she let out a small laugh.

"Oh, that's funny?"

She looked back at me. "Hell yeah. That's what his ass gets."

"Whatever." I said in disgust. Then, I knew exactly where I had heard her name before. It was when I was inside Malik's office. My head lazily turned to the ladies as I uttered in displeasure, "Well, I guess you ladies have just started another war."

"Why, Mike?" Tameia asked, eyes about to bulge out of her small ass head.

"For you girls who didn't know. That was the sister of Malik. The same damn guy who owns the club you guys just danced at."

"What?" Entyce asked in sheer shock and disappointment with herself.

"Yes, I heard him earlier talking on the phone about the disappearance."

"Damn! It seems like just as you guys get rid of one problem, another one pops the fuck up!" Mo Money recited as she stood there, just as shocked as we all were.

"Exactly! Oh well, let's ride." I uttered, while shaking my head, wondering what in the hell had we all gotten ourselves involved in.

Chapter 16
World Famous!

Things were definitely about to become complicated as I pondered back to the first time I saw that kid with the play dick shoved up his narrow ass. Him and a few of his other homies were the ones who had had their way with Strawberry only a few weeks ago. Damn, how about that? The same guy involved with me and the girls a second time. Only this time he met his untimely death. *What a horrible way to go*, I thought as Nicole slid her hand into mine.

She whispered softly into my ear. "Are you okay?"

I heard her sensuous voice which brought me back to reality. "You know that one guy, Punkin, was one of the guys that had did what they did to Strawberry, right?"

She looked up at me, face holding on to a distant stare. "Yeah, okay."

"Well, now that he's dead, what do you think the other guys that were with him that night are going to think when they all find out that his ass is dead?"

"So, you think that they're going to assume that we had something to do with it?"

"Precisely."

She looked away from me, now with her head held down. "What? You have nothing to say now, huh?"

She slowly lifted her head back up, then uttered, "You know what we do and what we're all capable of. So whatever happens, know that we don't back down from shit! Now let's go get some fucking sleep!"

"You heard her ass! Let's go, nigga!" Mo Money chimed in as she stuck her head around the corner.

"Alright, let's hope and pray that we're ready for whatever then," I replied as I walked to the driver's door of my truck.

As soon as I stepped inside, Suga Bear yelled out from the backseat. "Damn, Mike, did somebody die or something?"

My face immediately held a smirk as I looked into my rearview mirror. "I really don't know, Suga Bear. I mean Step."

"Alright, Mike."

"Yeah, my bad."

"Whatever. The reason I asked you was only due to the way you and a few of the girls stood outside, looking like y'all were planning a funeral for somebody."

I was just pulling out of the parking lot, following behind Mignon as I said, "Whatever, Step. We were just showing a lil' concern for the young lady; that's all."

"Okay," she replied as we pulled up at the red light.

My head then cunningly turned in the direction of Nicole, who I guess was daydreaming or thinking about what was to come. "Nicole!"

She jumped as if she was startled, looking at me with those big, sexy eyes of hers. "Yeah, bae," she hastily answered.

"Why in the hell are we driving away from the hotel we usually stay at?" I asked her with a quizzical look on my face.

"Mike, I told you inside Denny's. That's why we were all here in Jacksonville. Those dudes were the ones who paid for us to stay over at the Red Roof Inn."

"I see." I eased into my seat, getting ready for the ride to wherever in the hell they had them residing at for the weekend. As we drove away from Denny's that early morning, it dawned on me that Jacksonville was the biggest city in Florida, and for some strange reason everyone was connected with one another. It would be years later that I would find out that my man Malik knew just about every person that I or we would come in contact with. Florida was a very large state and I was about to find out just how large it really was when it came to the world famous Florida Hot Girls.

***

Firstborn had just passed the first Lake City exit, headed back to Madison, Florida, musing about all of the money he was about to be making from selling some of the best White Girl this side of Miami, Florida. The first thing that came to mind was where would he house all of the product that he had and then who would he get to help him distribute the purest cocaine that the small town of Madison would ever see.

The first person that came to mind was his cookie-shaped face cousin they called Chai, who by far was your average country ass brother, who already had his life in check. He worked a regular nine to five job where he was a fulltime supervisor at one of the largest local chicken plants in Florida. He was already making good money over at Goldkist, so why would he risk that for selling some powder?

Then there was Chai's brother, Richard. A big, light skinned brother who lived in Tallahassee. He too held a very lucrative job where he was working at a nice seafood restaurant, where just like his brother, was the daytime supervisor. So those two cousins of his would definitely not fit his scheme of things.

He then thought about a few of his close relatives that didn't have jobs, but could he trust them? He pondered over that as he passed the I-75 exit, smiling to himself as the possibility of all the fortune and fame he would inherit from being the top dawg in his small country town that he called home. As he continued driving, doing the required speed limit, he didn't even think to stop and grab a bite to eat. He was just so bent on getting back to Madison so that he could get things cracking. Then, as if a bolt of lightning had struck the top of his head, it hit him. The two people he thought he could get to move the precious product and help get his small business off the ground. Twan and his younger brother Fabian— two knuckle heads from back in the day. Two brothers that eventually grew up to become two of Madison's most talked about and feared individuals that the town had ever known.

The criminal-minded brothers were actually the brothers of this beautiful lil' redbone with the cutest hazel eyes that I had ever seen by the name of Deidra. I'd met her back in the early nineties and had fallen head over heels in love with her. At that time, her brothers were just two young men who still had breast milk on their breath. Now some years later, they had grown into two hungry young men who would relish in the business that my damn brother was about to create. And my brother had just what they needed to help them quench their hunger and thirst.

As he sped past the Lee exit, his face held a sinister smile as he thought that as soon as he hit Madison's city limits, he would go by their house and introduce them to what he had. If he only knew what he was about to get them all into, he might have never introduced them to that particular wild and crazy lifestyle.

Chapter 17
Their Death Was Inevitable!

That Sunday morning seemed like it came just as soon as I laid my head down to get some sleep. As I laid there in that king sized bed, thinking about taking Nicole and Mo Money for round two, I was just about to roll Mo Money's ass into a nice fucking position when I happened to hear the morning news on the television. They were reporting what had took place in the wee hours of the morning. The good news was that they had no witnesses or any information of what had all transpired. All they knew was that something drastic had taken place and they had no possible leads into their ongoing investigation.

I took a deep sigh of relief. As if the sky had fallen on top of my head, the damn lady reporter was interrupted by one of the officers who told her something. "Wait a minute, Stu! We have just been told that there is one lone survivor who might be able to help with this horrific crime scene!" she shouted back to the news anchor, who then really put a damper on my morning when the gotdamn man asked her, "Well, Angelia, do the police think that these murders are connected to the ones that happened about two weeks ago?"

"Ahhh, hell naw!" I shouted as I rose up in bed, waking Nicole and Mo Money up out of their deep slumber.

"They don't know right now, but when we do find out, we will be right there to report on it. There is one small problem with the lone victim here though, Stu."

"What's that?"

"It seems as though the man is on so much pain medication that he hadn't opened up his eyes as of yet. And the doctors have no idea when he would be able to open them or even if he could help the police solve the hideous crime," she said as my mouth dropped.

Now, not wanting to hear anything else about what had taken place, I just so happened to turn down the news, as Mo Money turned her naked body over and placed her arm on my chest. "Morning, Michael. You are up mighty early," she said, with her breath smelling just like pancakes and syrup.

I sat up in bed, staring back at her, not even seeing a picture of Rhynyia and her family on the television screen. It seemed as though they were reporting on the very same plane that we were on, but my stupid ass was too busy staring at Mo Money. "What's up, sexy? How did you sleep?" I was gazing at how nice her breast looked as they laid there, naked on her chest.

She yawned, then stretched. "Hell, after you put me and my girl to sleep, I guess I slept like a newborn baby, with a full stomach."

Nicole rolled over and said, "Yeah, you did that, bae. Now, do you two mind if I can get back to my dream?"

Mo Money pulled her pillow from up under her head and smacked Nicole across the face, grinning as she shouted, "Hoe, get that ass up! We have to go take a shower before we get ready to leave."

"Alright, bitch, that same word is what got Lil' Kitty that black eye early this morning!"

"Oh yeah, my bad!" Mo Money recited as she lightly smiled at Nicole and I.

"No problem, hoe." Nicole laughed.

"See, you need to stop playing. Now, get up so we can take a shower together."

"Ah shit, it's time to get up already?"

"Yep, so you two go ahead and get yourselves a shower," I said to them as I went back to watching the news.

Mo Money then tried kissing me in my mouth, by pulling my head in her direction. Without thinking I quickly yanked my head back towards the television. "Damn, Michael, you're watching the news as though you had something to do with what happened!"

"Why would you say something like that, young lady?" I asked as I continued looking away from her. I guess she must have heard about the incident at the warehouse on the news as well. But what I was watching was a replica of the plane Pierre had. If only I could have known what they were talking about. So, I turned the volume back up, hoping I could catch the tail end of what they were reporting on.

"Because, boo, I'm laying here butt ass naked and you're not even looking at me. Your ass is staring at that T.V. as if something is wrong."

"No, gorgeous, I'm just curious as to what happened, that's all," I said as I pulled her naked body close to me.

Just as she had nudged up against me, Nicole slid her head up under the sheets, then placed her warm mouth on my manhood, causing ole Johnboy to rise to the occasion. Just as she had him at attention, she blurted out, "Let me show you how much I've missed your black ass!"

Mo Money saw what was taking place and quickly snapped her head around. "Oh no, hoe, let me show his ass how we both missed him!"

Seconds later, they had my erected manhood between themselves as I laid back in bed with my hands crossed behind the back of my head. When my eyes closed, they knew they had my approval. "Y'all, go ahead and do what cha like."

Their heads were bobbing as if they were involved in an apple bobbing contest with me enjoying the attention I was getting, forgetting about what was just said on the news— which I should have been trying to do, since they had been reporting on a plane owned by Pierre Santiago that had eluded police helicopters by flying over the Bermuda Triangle.

***

Meanwhile, inside the room of the other ladies, they were just getting themselves ready when Chanel yelled out, "Alright, Chazz, it's already ten thirty and you know it's like three more of us girls out here that need to take a shower!"

"I'll be out in about two more minutes, Chanel. So, if you want to come in here with me, that's fine!" Chazz shouted back to Chanel who wanted to get inside the shower next.

"Girl, don't try me. You know damn well that I'm strictly dickly!" she shouted back at Chazz, who was drying off.

"Chanel, please, girl. I know how you feel about girls on girls, so please don't think that I was trying you in any kind of way. I was just trying to get you in the shower so you wouldn't be late."

"I'm good. Thank you, Chazz," Chanel voiced while marching into the bathroom.

"I don't know why you feed into her nonsense," Tarshay said to Chazz while brushing her hair.

"I don't. I was just trying to be helpful, that's all."

"I know, Chazz, but as long as you're in this group, always worry about you first. 'Cause it's some shady ass females in this group that don't give a damn about nobody but themselves."

"She ain't lying, girl!" Lil' Kitty said while eating on the rest of her leftovers, looking sad and beaten down as she slowly chewed on what was left.

"Umph, thanks, girl. How is your eye?" Chazz asked, trying her best not to stare at the awful thing.

Lil' Kitty soberly walked over to the trash can and placed the empty plate in the garbage, then looked in the mirror at her eye. "It's okay. I just hope it goes down before we get home."

"I seriously doubt that one, honey," Chazz recited as she slid on a sexy pair of thongs, then her outfit.

***

Over in the room that the Murder Queens shared…

"So, Mignon, what time do you think we'll be back in Orlando?"

"It all depends on how fast Mike and the rest of us are driving, Strawberry. Why? Do you have something to do when we get back?" Mignon asked Strawberry while placing mascara on her face.

"Nah, but if the news reporters are correct in what their saying, we all might want to be leaving here real fucking fast!"

Mignon hastily turned around and looked at Strawberry before she asked her, "What in the hell are you talking about, Strawberry?"

Strawberry then turned up the volume on the television, causing the noise to wake up Entyce. "Look!" Strawberry shouted with astonishment in her face and voice.

Mignon then yelled over to Tameia who was in the bathroom finishing up her shower. "Tameia, hurry the fuck up! You might want to come out here and check this shit out!"

By now Entyce had sat up in bed, watching what they were all seeing on the screen.

"Oh my God, I wonder if Mike is watching this shit, too?" Strawberry asked the girls, who were all glued to what was being said on the screen.

Moments later, Mignon was calling over to my room with concern. I saw that it was her and answered on the first ring.

"Hello."

"Hey, Mike, are you up yet?" she asked with a bit of panic in her voice.

"Yes, Mignon. Why? What's up now?"

"They found a body, Mike!" she expressed as the distress in her voice amplified through my ears.

"I know, Mignon. First, just calm down. Everything is going to be okay. Just finish doing what you all are doing and be ready to leave at noon. The important thing to do is just act like nothing's wrong; do you understand?"

"Yes, Mike." She sounded calm and collected.

"Cool."

"How can you remain so calm and cool at a moment like this?" she asked.

"It's what I do: stay calm at moments like this." I was still on the phone with Mignon when Nicole and Mo Money walked out of the bathroom together in nothing but their birthday suits.

"Alright, Mike, are you okay?" Mignon asked.

I stood there observing the two naked vixens before me. "Yes, I'm fine. Give me a minute to get ready. Check on the rest of the girls and I'll see you in a few. Oh, and make sure Richard and his crew of girls are ready also."

"Yes, Mike, will do. I'll see you then."

We hung up with Mo Money draped around my back. She then playfully peaked her head around my waist as she looked up into my face and said, "We were hoping that you would've at least joined us in the shower. But we see that you were busy handling business."

"Indeed, that I was, young lady." I spoke while planting a kiss on her forehead and then walking into the bathroom so that I could take myself a shower. I knew that time was of the essence and we had to be leaving soon.

"Is everything okay, Michael?" Nicole asked as she stepped in front of me, hindering me from entering the bathroom.

I kindly gave her a warm, gentle smile before saying, "I really don't know, but I guess we will all find out in a little while."

"Damn, that serious, huh?"

"Who knows?" I answered as she leaned forward, asking for her morning kiss.

Chapter 18
Mind Pondering!

Seconds later I was inside the shower before my towel hit the ceramic tile floor. I lazily turned the water on hot then placed my back underneath the pulsating vapors to relieve myself of the stress from the previous night's events. As I stood there with the water streaming down my body, the thoughts of Rhynyia and Firstborn raced through my mind. Now here it was that I was pondering if they made it back home safe and sound, and if so, why hadn't either one of them called me as of yet? I specifically instructed Rhynyia to call me as soon as they flew over the Atlantic Ocean, with my brother being instructed to return the rental just as soon as he touched down in Madison. And if he ran into any problems to call me immediately. As I stood there thinking of him and all of that weight, why in the hell would I tell his black ass to call me if something happened? For if he did, there was no way in hell that I was going down the road with him with all of that dope. Don't get me wrong, I loved my brother truly, but when and if he got caught with all of that product, his black ass was going to be up Schitt's Creek without a paddle. And I wanted no parts of it, no matter what.

Just as I turned around, Mo Money was busy knocking at the bathroom door with another surprise waiting on me. "Yeah, what is it?" I yelled.

"Your phone is ringing!" she shouted back while placing her make-up on.

"Who is it?"

"The screen says someone by the name of Sharon!" she screamed from behind the bathroom door.

Damn. How in the hell did I forget to call her? She was one of the most important females in my life at that time besides Rhynyia. Without wanting her or Nicole to answer it, due to me being afraid of what they might say to her, I quickly jumped out of the shower and grabbed my phone. Just as I reached it, I had to control my breathing. "Hello?"

"Damn, nigga, you can't call me like you said you would?" she asked with an unusual tone in her voice.

"Sharon, wait a minute! Why do you have to talk to me with such anger in your voice?" I could tell that something was troubling her by the tone she had with me.

"First of all, Michael, you take your black ass out of town without even seeing me before your tired ass left, not knowing if I was dead or alive. Then you neglect calling me the entire time that you were over there with your side chick. Just leaving your baby and I here to do for ourselves!"

She was absolutely right; I did leave without seeing her. Hell, when I left, she was still in the hospital sleeping as if she wasn't waking up any time soon. Her comments left me standing there partially naked, staring at my reflection in the mirror. I was practically speechless.

"Hello! Say something, Michael!"

I took a moment then sighed. "You're right, Sharon, and I'm sorry. As soon as I get back home, I'm coming over to your place so that I can spend some quality time with you and the baby."

"Forget that, Michael! Quality time is what got my lil' red ass knocked the fuck up with your baby! You know what I want?"

My head fell aimlessly into my hand as I silently asked her, "No, Sharon. What is it that you want?"

I could hear her in the background as she began to sob, when her friend took the phone from her hand. "Hello, Michael."

"Yes, who is this?"

"It's her girlfriend, Maxine," the tender voice uttered.

"Oh, hi."

"Hello to you as well, Michael. Listen, I don't know if you knew this or had even heard over the news yet."

I was walking over to the bed, knowing damn well that Sharon hadn't seen the news up in Jacksonville about the killings over at the warehouse. So, I played it off by saying, "No, I haven't. What happened?"

"Sharon shot and killed that crooked cop, Lt. Richards last night!"

"What?" I asked, sounding hysterical.

"Yes, it seems as though it wasn't him that was found dead at the hospital. It was his partner. Somehow, he found his way over to Sharon's house last night and tried to kill her. But my girl was one step ahead of him and caught the son of a bitch off guard, killing the bastard with three shots. Two to his chest and one to his head."

As I fell to the bed in disbelief, Mo Money stood there silently listening with her hands on her hips. "So, is she okay?" I asked while staring at Mo Money who was looking down at me.

"Yes, Michael, but she needs you more than anything right about now."

"I understand. I'm in Jacksonville right now. I should be home in the next few hours. Once I get there, I'll be by to see her," I said, really not knowing what to do or even what to say.

"Hold on, Michael, she wants to speak back to you."

"Sure."

I could hear Maxine hand the phone back over to Sharon as she dully came back over the phone. Her voice sounded like she had just finished crying as she sputtered, "Michael."

"Yes, boo. I'm so sorry. As soon as I get home, I'm coming over to see you." As soon as I uttered those sentiments, Mo Money rolled her cute praline eyes at me and fleetly walked up out of the room in a hurry. Angry I presumed. Nicole, who had been sitting patiently, just looked at her leave, then back at me as she shrugged her shoulders.

"Michael, I want more than that. I need to come stay with you for a few days. My house has been like a circus since last night."

"I do understand, Sharon. Pack a few things and I'll be there to pick you and Breanna up. And once again, I'm so sorry about what happened with you last night."

"No problem, bae. Oh, and one more thing," she said before I could hang up.

"Yeah, what's up?" I should have never asked her that, because what she was about to ask me next caused my heart to drop. It was as if the words had come out of her mouth slowly because I heard everything, twice.

"Everything happened so fast last night. One minute I was on the phone with my mother who was trying to tell me about her other daughter who she had before me!"

"What?" I asked, cutting her off in mid sentence.

"Yes. And get this, Michael. She was trying to tell me that you might even know who she is!"

Now I was really about to have a very bad day as I stood up to march over to the window of my room, while Nicole stood near the door. Shaken by the terrible news and the idea of Karen, Rhynyia's mother, saying something to Sharon about her other daughter, I placed my hand over my phone and said to Nicole, "Go find that damn girl before she runs out into traffic or something!"

"Do you think that she would do something like that?" Nicole asked as she reached for the doorknob.

"Hell yeah, now please go get her!" I spat while Sharon shouted through the phone.

"Michael, did you hear what I said?"

"Yes, I did. I wonder what makes your mother think something like that?" I asked as I frantically began pacing the room.

"I have no idea. I was just going to wait until you got back so we could go ask her together."

"Damn," I said under my voice.

"What was that, baby?"

"Nothing. I tell you what. Let me get in the shower so I can get ready to leave. We'll talk about this when I get over there."

"Okay, bae. Be safe," she said as I was trying to get off the phone.

"Alright, I'll see you soon."

"Michael."

"Yes, Sharon."

"I love you," she uttered as I could hear the sincerity in her voice.

Then my black ass goes and says something to her that I should have never said knowing damn well that I had just proposed to Rhynyia only a few days ago. "No, Sharon, I love you more."

"Whatever, Michael," she said as I could practically hear her smiling through her phone.

"Alright, boo, I'm about to start packing a few things right now."

As soon as I placed my phone down, Nicole and Mo Money walked back in the room with Mo Money's face holding on to a sad smile.

"Hey, you. Listen. There are some things that I have to take care of once we get back to Orlando, so please try to understand and don't act like that. But I'm going to need for you to fall back for a few days or so." She looked at me with hot tears in the well of her eyes. "Just until I handle some business."

She grayly walked over to her bags then looked back at me with her soft eyes. "I guess the ladies were right about you, huh, Michael?"

I walked over to her and tried to pull her into my arms, but she pulled away. "Hey, stop that, girl. It isn't like that."

"Whatever, Michael. Once we get home, I'll be replaced with the chick who you just got off the phone with!"

"Girl, stop. That was someone totally different."

Nicole then reached in and took her by the hand. "He serious, Mo. It's just his lil' girlfriend, that's all. Hell, I have to deal with that one or the one his ass just came back from Puerto Rico visiting with." Her face revealed a wicked smirk as she explained.

"Whatever. So I'm supposed to be girlfriend number four or five, Michael?"

"No, it's not that serious, young lady."

"Michael, I heard you tell her that you loved her."

"See, that's what you get for eavesdropping."

She stood there for a brief moment, then turned to walk out the door with her bags. Just as she placed her hand back on the doorknob, she numbly turned around and said something to me that still stays with me until this very day. "I hope that poor girl realizes that the only thing you really love, Michael Vallentino, is the Florida Hot Girls!" She then snatched open the door and stomped out.

My head quickly turned to Nicole who placed her head down, then looked up at me. "She's right, Michael. If there's one thing that you love more than life itself, is the fact that you own the Florida Hot Girls."

Chapter 19

Her Secret!

As Nicole left and went after her again, I wearisomely turned to stare at the reflection in the mirror that looked back at me. And for the third time in my life, I couldn't or didn't recognize the person that was looking back at me. Mo Money was right. I was truly in love with the idea of having a group of beautiful, exotic women in my life that were in popular demand all throughout the Sunshine State. Nothing— I mean nothing— was going to come between us as their fame and popularity began to blossom.

But if I would have only listened to my parents in the very beginning, I would have dropped them females so damn quick that they wouldn't have ever seen it coming. But no, here I am, and where are they?

By now, the group of females that I had assembled were not only turning heads, they were actually breaking necks. That's right, they were a group of women who demanded mad attention wherever and whenever they stepped into any building or bachelor party. And the good thing about it was the fact that they enjoyed the attention more than their fans did. So, you see, there wasn't any room or time for me to give that special female all of my quality time. While walking out of that hotel room that Sunday morning with my bags in my hand, I couldn't help but wonder how I would handle Sharon and her daughter staying with me for a few days? A part of me wished that I wouldn't have invited her and her young child over, due to me becoming bored with sleeping with the same woman every night. A phase that I had been going through ever since leaving my ex-wife Camisha. But just as I hit the door of my room, I remembered what Sharon had said about her mother wanting to tell her about her older sister. Instantly I stopped walking and immediately pulled out my cell phone to dial her number.

She answered on the first ring; her voice sounding as if she was a nervous wreck. "Hello? Is this you, Michael?"

"Yes, ma'am. How are you doing?" I asked, not really giving a fuck since she was about to let the cat out of the bag by revealing Rhynyia to Sharon.

"I'm fine. Just about to go over to Sharon's place to make sure that she's okay. Did you hear about what happened last night?"

"Yes, ma'am. I just found out after a very long conversation with her."

"How is she?" her mother asked, acting like she didn't already know how she was doing.

"She's fine, ma'am." I replied, then cut right to the chase with. "But why were you about to tell her about your first child? I thought you wanted me to find her father then tell you where he was?"

"I know where he is. I just wasn't sure how I was going to break the news about Rhynyia to Sharon since you're sleeping with both of my daughters."

Well Damn! She had to go there, I said to myself. "I know how it must seem, Karen, but rest assured, I was eventually going to let them both know what was going on. Just let me handle this my way, please."

"Your way, huh?" she uttered with a bit of sarcasm in her voice.

"Yes, ma'am."

"I see. Well, did you meet her father while over in Puerto Rico?" she asked.

"Yes, ma'am, and trust me, he is the man you said that he was."

"I know, that's why I have to keep my whereabouts a secret to him and his powerful family."

"I do understand, so you can understand where I stand also?"

"Yes, Michael. I promise to keep what you have going on between you and me. All I ask Michael, is that you not hurt either one of my children. But know this, one day you're going to have to choose between the two of them. And that's one day that I surely hope to never see. Because my Sharon really loves you with all of her heart, just like I know Rhynyia does," she spoke sincerely to me, causing my heart to drop to my stomach.

"I know and trust me; I will handle this situation that I'm in very carefully. But Ms. Karen, while I have you on the phone, let me ask you something?"

"Go ahead, Michael."

"Your father, Sharon and Rhynyia's grandfather."

"What about my father?"

"Did you all ever find out how did his accident take place? While over in Puerto Rico, Rhynyia spoke briefly on what might have happened," I spoke.

"You know Michael, the police wrote it off as a terrible traffic accident, but I think there was foul play involved."

"You know, so do I," I uttered as she came back with.

"How so?" She asked as I felt intrigued to fill her in on what I assumed.

***

It was around twelve forty-five before all of the ladies and I were leaving the hotel that Sunday afternoon. Richard had all of his ladies inside his truck ready to go as I tiresomely stumbled toward my truck, still stuck on what Mo Money had expressed to me, right before she stormed out of my room, earlier. The temperature was around eighty-five degrees with clear blue skies as the females that were riding with me, amusingly climbed into the truck, ready to take that long, hot ride back to Orlando.

Nicole sat right next to me as Mo Money sat by the door, still not looking the same as she did the night before.

"How is she doing?" I asked Nicole, while sitting there trying to figure her mood out.

"She's fine. I was able to calm her down a bit." Nicole spoke softly as she stared into my eyes. I swear, every time her gorgeous ass looked at me, melted my heart. I knew right then and there, if we were to have a girl, like my previous children were, that girl was going to melt my heart every time I looked into her precious little eyes.

"Thanks, I owe you one," I recited as I looked at Nicole, then gave her a wink.

"Yes, you do. More than just one," she replied as she smiled back.

Then, I shouted to the ladies, "Excuse me, ladies! Give me a quick minute while I speak with Mignon and her crew of ladies!" The ladies that were already inside of her truck were just getting themselves seated when Tameia spotted me walking in their direction.

"Hey, ladies. Here comes, Mike. I wonder what his ass wants now," she said as she adjusted her seatbelt.

Mignon then slid down her window as I stuck my head inside and spoke.

"Hey, listen, we all know that we have a slight problem since you guys left one of them thugs alive?"

"Yeah, we know, Mike," Strawberry said from the rear seat, then turning her wide ass nose up as if I was holding them up.

"Okay, so you all know what that means? I'm going to need you ladies to stay here and take care of our small problem. Once you ladies are done, meet the rest of us at Apollo South."

"Club Apollo!" Entyce uttered as she slid up in her seat.

"Yes, that's where the girls and I will be later on tonight. You ladies do know that today is Sunday, right?"

"My bad, Mike. I forgot all about that club," Entyce recited.

"No problem, ladies. So do what it is you girls do best, and we'll hook up there," I said to them as I hit the door of the truck with my fist, then gave Mignon the peace sign.

"Will do, Mike. We'll see you later," Mignon said to me as she began to put her truck in reverse, but just as she put the truck in drive, Nicole shot up from the rear screaming out loudly.

"Hey! Hey! Hold up!"

Mignon quickly snapped her head around to see her girl sprinting up the vehicle, practically out of breath. "Girl, you almost got your lil' ass ran the fuck over! Now what's wrong?" Mignon asked her.

"I guess you guys must have forgotten about the car?" She asked, while trying to catch her breath, then placing her hands on her waist. She was now breathing slowly as she tried to keep her composure.

"What car? What is she talking about, Mignon?" I asked as I stood there looking at the women inside the truck.

"Oh shit! I forgot all about that damn car!" Mignon uttered as she looked across the street.

Then, ploddingly turning my head in the direction of where Mignon's eyes were staring, I witnessed what I didn't want to see. "What the fuck?" came out of my mouth as I peered over at the lime green Chevy parked across the street from the hotel.

Chapter 20
Lime Green!

I quickly snapped back around to Mignon, who was looking at me very confused. "Okay, so who car is that and is there someone inside?"

She cleared her throat. "No, Mike, there's no one inside."

"Okay, so who does it belong to, if I may ask the million-dollar question?"

Without any hesitation at all, she says, "That's Punkin's car! We had to drive it here after we stashed his small ass over at that warehouse," Tameia voiced as she eased up in her seat.

"Okay, so please tell me what in the hell are we going to do with it here?"

"It's all good, Mike. Just as soon as you all pull out from the hotel, I'll have Tameia follow us in the car and have it disposed of."

"Sounds good," I replied, knowing that my girls would make sure not leave any evidence behind that would connect them or rather me and them to the hideous crime that we had did.

"So where are you guys going now?" Nicole asked as she stood next to me, talking with Mignon.

"Someone has to handle our problem of the lone survivor left behind."

"Oh snap, do you guys need me, too?" Nicole asked.

"Yeah, go ahead and hop in," Mignon spat.

"Cool," she said, then right after she sat down, she looked out to me and said, "Hey, Mike, send Mo Money over here, too."

"Damn, you guys have done a lot of recruiting since I've been gone."

With a great big smile on her face, Mignon recited, "Yes, we have, and I must say, they have been a great addition to the team."

"Is that so?" I asked as I smiled back at her, then moved towards the front of the truck. "Hey, Mo Money! Could I see you for a minute, please?"

Her head went down as she bluntly opened the door, then walked over to where I was standing. "Yes, Mike?"

"Hey, hold your damn head up and stop acting like I have stepped all over your heart!"

"Whatever, Mike. What do you want?" She asked as she tried to look away from me.

I placed my hand up under her chin, slowly lifting her face so I could see her. "It's not me. It's the crew of ladies that you have joined who need you."

"Oh, what's hood ladies?" She asked as a jolly looking expression magically appeared on her face.

"Hey, we're going to need your assistance with what we have going on, if you don't mind," Nicole uttered as she stuck her head out of the window.

It didn't take Mo Money no time at all to answer as she quickly shouted back. "About damn time. Hell yeah, I'm all in! Let's ride!" She eagerly went to the door where her dear pal Nicole was seated. She had just reached for the door of the truck when she turned back to me and said, "And you better not be fucking any of them hoes in your truck, my nigga!" She gave me a shy smile, then stepped inside of the truck, ready to go.

"Whatever, Mo Money. You guys be safe," I replied as I gingerly began to walk back over to my truck with hopes of the ladies taking care of some unfinished business before it landed us all inside someone's prison.

Moments later, I was back inside my truck, when I could hear Chyna' s mouth. "So, Mike, where are they going?"

"They had some things to take care of before leaving. Is that okay with you, Chyna?"

"Yeah, I guess so. It's not me asking," she quickly said as she climbed her sexy ass into the front seat.

"Well, who wants to know, Chyna?" I asked as I looked over at her and them mouthwatering breast of hers. Hands down, Chyna had to have the most precious looking titties my young ass had ever seen. For a moment there, I actually wanted to have the left one inside my mouth and me pretending to be a baby all over again.

She broke my attention when she turned her head and said, "It was your girl, Lil' Kitty."

"What?" I asked her as I turned my head to the rear of my truck because I knew damn well she wasn't inside.

"It was Lil' Kitty. She's over in Richard's truck, talking about the car across the street. Something about it belongs to her nigga Punkin and she believes he was here at the hotel seeing one of us girls."

"Oh, yeah?" I asked as I turned the key in the ignition.

"Yep, she's on the phone right now. Here!" Chyna spoke as she handed me her phone.

"Hello?"

"Mike, is one of them hoes in that truck sleeping with my man Punkin?" She asked in her squeaky ass voice.

I sighed then replied. "Lil Kitty, please. Every man out of town is not your man. And how would I know who the man is fucking?"

"I'm just saying, because his car is parked across from the hotel he paid for," she yelped.

"Just because the man's car is here doesn't mean that he's here, Lil' Kitty," I replied, trying my best to contain my knowledge of what really had happened to the damn guy.

Then it dawned on me. The simple fact was that what if the homicide detectives that were assigned to the case got a hold of his cellphone and somehow connected Lil' Kitty and the entire events of the weekend back to my fucking girls? *Damn, this fucking bitch!* I mumbled to myself with her rambling in my ear. "Lil Kitty, girl please stop! Just lay back and chill. We all have a long ride back to Orlando, and when we get back, you might need to take your black ass a short vacation!"

"But why?" she asked, sounding as if she was about to cry.

"Because I said so! Now get off my phone!"

***

Mignon and the Murder Queens were at the hospital, where their lone victim lay in bed, fast asleep from all of the pain medication that the many doctors had him on. The women were all in position as the clock had just struck two in the afternoon, that somewhat hot, blistering day. Their time of executing their plan of attack was just around the time the city was making preparations for the Super Bowl. Their victim had limited security as Strawberry and Entyce walked down to the Intensive Care Unit, pretending to be nurses. They had just got a few steps away from their victim as they stood still and unnoticed; while keeping a watchful eye on the two police officers standing outside of the man's room.

The closer they got to his room, the more they could hear from the officer's boring conversation, complaining about the time and how they couldn't wait to get off. Meanwhile, sitting over in the visitation portion of the Intensive Care Unit, Mo Money pretended to be waiting on a dear sick relative herself as she sat there watching the victim's older brother, Lil' Breezy. Next to the side of Lil' Breezy was a heavy-set woman who Mo Money assumed was their mother. It didn't matter though, because just as soon as either one of them would have got out of pocket, she was prepared to take both of them out, right there in that small, cramped room.

Lil Breezy had just got into town from North Carolina. He was supposed to have met up with the guys at the warehouse, but for some reason his older cousin, Breezy, had linked up with some trick from the club and wasn't in place. Good for them both, because if they would have been at the warehouse, they might have met the same fate as Lil' Breezy ' s brother and friends. While Mo Money sat there in that room, for some odd reason she got the uncanny feeling that she was being watched. So, she eased her light brown eyes up from the magazine she was reading, to lock eyes with Lil' Breezy. Just as she gazed up at the man, he hit her with.

"What's up lil' mama?"

She played him off by pointing at herself, then asking, "Who me?"

"Yes, you are the only other person in here, aren't you?" He asked as she began to scan the waiting room.

"Oh yeah, I am. My bad. What's good with you?" She asked.

Him being the slick one, replied. "That's what I was about to ask you."

Down the corridor and about five minutes later, Mignon walked onto the same floor from the opposite direction. Quickly seeing that the coast was clear, she made a beeline towards Entyce and Strawberry at the end of the wing.

"So how many officers do they have on his door?" Mignon asked.

"It seems like two and by the way they're talking to one another it seems as if they have had enough of the babysitting role for the day," Strawberry replied while Mignon and her crew kept a keen eye on the prize.

"Perfect, that's all I need to hear. My plan should work out just fine."

As soon as she uttered those daunting words, the elevator door went *Ping!*

Two beautiful, I mean gorgeous black females, dressed as cops, stepped off of the elevator. They both surveyed the corridor, making their entrance look real, then walked straight to the room of their victim, Marquise. The one very large white officer abruptly turned his fat ass neck around, that held up his small head, when his wide nose caught the nice smelling fragrance of the expensive perfume that Nicole wore. This caused a wide smile to appear on the man's face as he grabbed at his manhood, when he witnessed the pair walking their way.

He stood shit faced for a few seconds, then frantically wiping away the crumbs from his Bear Claw doughnut that were smeared about his face.

"Well, hello there, officers," he spoke as his words seemed to stutter as he stood there gazing at their beauty.

"Hello to you as well," Nicole said while smiling at the man. "I'm Officer Johnson and this is my partner, Officer Williams. We're the two relief officers for today's shift," Nicole recited as the officer couldn't keep his wandering eyes off of her shapely breasts staring back at him inside of her fifty-dollar police stripper outfit. It made them look just like some real professional police officers.

"Wow, may I ask what precinct you two ladies are from?" Officer Murray asked as he stood there next to his partner.

"Southside," Tameia blurted out without even thinking, brushing up against the black, bald officer standing there next to Officer Bryan Craze. The tingling sensation instantly caused officer Murray to become nervous and unhinged as he began to fidget around when Tameia brushed up against him, slightly causing the bald brother to stumble backwards, almost falling over his own two left feet.

Chapter 21
Actual Officers!

The moment was funny as Mignon and Strawberry stood far away, laughing at how clumsy and stupid the two officers of the law looked.

"Be quiet girl, they might hear us!" Mignon said to Strawberry, who quickly wiped away her smile and then looked at the back of Mignon.

"That's your silly ass, laughing all loud and shit! I'm cool."

"Whatever," Mignon said as she turned to gaze back at Strawberry.

"Shh, I can't hear what they're saying," Strawberry uttered as Mignon turned back in time to hear Tameia ask.

"So how is our witness doing?" she asked as she wore her outfit like a fucking glove.

"Ahh, he hasn't woke up as of yet, but I'm pretty sure his ass will when he smells how nice you two smell. If I didn't know any better, I would swear that you ladies look like y'all just came from the club," Officer Craze muttered.

"Exactly, like a strip club or something," Officer Murray chimed in with, as he stood there not being shy at all. Not even realizing that his bald head ass was staring directly at Nicole's protruding pussy print.

"Oh really, now why would you think something like that?" Nicole asked, while becoming agitated by the way Officer Murray continued staring at what he couldn't have, even if he was the last hard dick on the planet. The man was so engrossed at what his eyes were seeing that he wasn't even making eye contact with the gorgeous female.

"You know, I'm just saying that is all," Murray replied as his thick lips began to moisten at the sight of Nicole's print.

"Well, who's to say that we don't moonlight and work at one of the local strip clubs from time to time, big daddy," Nicole recited as she began to slowly rub on the bald head officer.

Now this is where things began to become awkward for the nine-year veteran on the force. Just as her soft hands touched the man, he started to shake as if he was having an orgasm, right there in front of everybody. His partner Craze saw that his partner was having a peculiar predicament as he quickly stepped in with.

"Hey Murray, the men's bathroom is down the hall to the right. You might want to go take care of yourself, good buddy!"

"Yeah, before you get all that shit all over the floor, causing one of these good nurses to slip and have a very dangerous fall," Nicole versed with her lips turned sideways.

The brother was embarrassed, I mean humiliated as he quickly placed his hands over the wet spot inside his pants, then saying out loud.

"Yeah, you're right! I don't know how in the hell that shit happened."

"Yeah right," Tameia said as she stood there shaking her head from side to side, then cutting a half smirk at the man.

"Okay, back to you, Officer Craze, it is right?" Nicole asked as she stepped a little closer to him.

"Yes, that's correct."

"Fine. Well, if you don't mind, my partner and I can handle things from here."

"You sure that you ladies are going to be okay, because I don't have nothing to do but go bike riding on my new Harley Davidson bike that I just purchased," Officer Craze uttered, while really trying to show Nicole why he had earned the nickname, Home Wrecker. A nickname that only the women who he would trick with from time to time, knew him by.

"Nah, we're good. You can go ahead and enjoy your free time. And oh, by the way, you might want to go check on your partner," Tameia voiced as they watched Officer Craze fleetly walk down to the men's bathroom.

"Thanks a million ladies, take care!" He shouted as he abruptly picked up two doughnuts for the road, then hurrying to check on his dear friend, Officer Murray.

As soon as the coast was clear, Mignon, Strawberry and Entyce walked down to the room, with their faces covered by surgical masks while leaving Tameia and Nicole outside, making it look like they were actual police officers. The door of the dim lighted room gently slid closed as Mignon took out her weapon and then carefully screwed on the silencer, while Strawberry did the same.

The angels above must have been watching over the large brother, because just as the ladies had their weapons ready and aimed to fire at his black rusty ass, his eyes sleepily began to open as he faintly tried to make out the faces standing before him.

Once his eyes focused in on the three females standing over him a single tear began to snake down his face as he softly uttered.

"Mom?" he faintly asked.

"Nah son, we're not your gotdamn mother. Consider us the bitches that you and your goons planned on raping and then killing!" Entyce mumbled with anger in her voice.

"I'm so sorry that things had to end like this, but just know that I never really meant to hurt any of you beautiful ladies."

He then tried to cry and think of what had caused all of this to happen in the first place.

"The feelings are mutual my dying brother, but you were the one who made it like this. So we're the ones who have to bring this all to an end. If only you would have left things alone, we wouldn't have had to hunt you down and kill you like the dog you really are!" Strawberry recited as she stood there with her semi-automatic weapon, zeroed in on his chest area.

"Damn, that's some cold-hearted shit there, lil' mama," he managed to say just as they all heard. *Pst-pst-pst-pst.*

Four rounds hissed like a mad female Cobra Snake as his large, framed body jerked every time one of the rounds tore off into his flesh. The four rounds from Strawberry's gun ripped through his chest.

Pst-pst-pst.

While three rounds of Mignon's weapon tore off the front portion of the man's frontal lobe.

Pst-pst-pst.

Then three more rounds hissed from the barrel of Entyce's gun as she looked over at Mignon, who was staring back at her. "Well, damn, bitch! Has your ass ever heard of overkill?"

"Yes, but I had to make sure that his chocolate ass didn't come back from the dead this time," Entyce replied as she placed her weapon back inside her pocket, then taking a very deep breath, then exhaling. Now as Entyce stood there, thinking of what him and his partners had in mind for them, Strawberry walked up behind her, placing bar hand on Entyce's shoulder.

"Damn bitch, by the way you just shot ole boy in his face, his big ass won't be eating on any more of them good ass barbecue ribs his ass be cooking!"

"Shut up hoe, how do you know about him cooking ribs and shit?" Entyce asked as they all turned to walk out of the door.

"Because the night them niggas took me out the club, they stopped by his rib shack," she replied, half smirk on her face.

"Well I be damned," Entyce said as they got to the door, but just when they were about to open the door, Nicole swiftly turned and shouted. "Hey, did you hoes get all of the shell casings?

"Oh shit, thanks for reminding us," Strawberry shouted as she went for the shell casings. While Strawberry did that, Mignon looked over to Nicole and said, "Go get Mo Money out of the waiting room."

"I'm on it," Nicole versed as she darted out of the room, making sure to check the hallway left and right before exiting the room. Even though they thought that they had killed their victim, they still had to make a clean getaway. Just as she got to the waiting room door, Lil' Breezy was seated next to Mo Money. He seen Nicole, just as she witnessed him. "Excuse me Officer, can we see him now?"

Nicole's pretty face held an evil grin as she uttered. "Right now might not be a good time. It seems as though he had a mild setback. Someone will be here momentarily to let the family know of his apparent status." Nicole then winked at Mo Money, who instantly knew what to do.

"Okay officer, thank you," Lil' Breezy said as he stood up and went to sit with the mother, trying his best to keep the woman from crying.

"No problem, sir. Have a nice day."

They were all halfway back down the hall when Mo Money asked Nicole, "So did you guys get him?"

Nicole wittingly looked over at her young protege in training and muttered. "Does a bear shit in the woods?"

"Hell, I don't know, I guess a bear can shit anywhere his ass wants too!" Mo Money replied as she smiled at Nicole, then stepped onto the elevator with the rest of the crew.

The team of dangerous, notorious women stepped on the elevator and all watched Strawberry push the button for the parking garage. "Did everyone make sure that everything you were told to do, went as told to you?"

Tameia sighed before saying, "Of course, Mignon, everything went as planned. Now do we have enough time to make it back to Orlando before we have to leave for Tampa?"

Nicole flipped over her wrist, gazing at her diamond studded time piece. Then, looked back up at Mignon. "Well by my watch, we should get back in good time. It all depends on the captain of the ship here!"

The women all turned their attention to Mignon, who looked back at them and said, "Hell, don't y'all all look at me. If any of you hoes feel like driving, I will be happy to sit my fine red ass in the back seat and get some rest, while one of you drive."

"Alright Mignon, you know what happened to Lil' Kitty for calling one of us a hoe?" Nicole stated as they all burst out into laughter, just as the elevator reached the parking garage.

"My bad, I'm so sorry, Mo Money. Believe me, I don't want no smoke."

Mo Money gave her a half smile, before saying, "Don't worry, girl, me neither."

The door quietly slid apart as two young familiar faces walked onto the elevator, just as the Murder Queens all stepped off. They were slightly covering their faces as they all stepped off, making sure they kept their backs to the two black gentleman. The two men were taken back for a minute as they walked off gazing at the bodies of the crew of women who walked right past them as if they didn't even know them. When the elevator door closed, the young man looked over at his partner and mumbled.

"Hey, Malik, when have you ever seen female police officers or hospital nurses, wearing three-inch Red Bottoms?"

Malik leaned back up against the elevator wall, taking everything in, while looking as if he was trying to remember where he had seen the gorgeous crew of women before. After a few moments he answered back with. "Come to think about it! Never, my young brother. If I didn't know any better, I would swear that those females were fucking strippers," he said while looking into the eyes of his club DJ. They two men were still staring at one another, when the door of the elevator opened up, where lay the dead corpse of the young man they had come to see, not knowing that they were just a few minutes too late.

When the door fully opened, both men caught police officers, family members and doctors running back and forth screaming and crying. Malik swiftly stepped off the elevator and grabbed Lil' Breezy and asked him. "Yo, dawg, what's going on?" Lil' Breezy was violently shaking as he looked into the cold red eyes of his friend, Malik. Then looking over at the woman he knew as a second mother to him. She was sprawled out over the floor screaming and shouting, showing her natural black ass as she shouted out loudly.

"Oh lardy, lawd! Why take another one of my precious babies? Why lawd, why?" Her eyes and face were drenched with her tears as she stared up into the ceiling as if an answer was about to fall to her.

This is when Lil' Breezy looked back at Malik and angrily shouted, "What in the fuck do you think happened, my nigga? Some police officer bitches just ran up in here and blew my fucking brother's face the fuck off!"

Malik looked back at his young partner and said, "I betcha ass that those bitches that we just passed back there in that elevator had something to do with this shit."

Chapter 22
Two Very Busy Days!

Firstborn drove back into the city limits of Madison, Florida around seven forty-five in the AM. He was still over excited and vamped up about what he had with him. The first thing he did was to stop by his family's house, which he shared with his aunt and mother. Not to mention the few nephews and nieces that slept throughout the large wood frame house, on top of one another, due to the small house being so heavily populated.

Once he stepped out of the rental, he quietly opened the front door of the old wood frame house and stood silent in the doorway; as he watched a few invited tenants, huge Cockroaches, damn near people size, run across the floor. One of the roaches even stopped dead in its tracks and looked him face to face, even had the nerve of asking him.

"Hey nigga, did you bring any food, cause there ain't a damn thing to eat up in this raggedy ass muthafucka?"

Firstborn just shrugged his shoulders and replied. "Hell nah muthafucka! And after today, y'all bitches have to leave!"

The huge Cockroach just looked back at him before uttering. "Fuck you and this raggedy ass house, we're leaving any damn way!"

He angrily closed the door, making sure not to wake up any of the people sleeping. Then mumbling to himself. "I'm so damn tired of these damn roaches, just makes me sick to my damn stomach. How they all live here and don't pay any fucking rent!" He then fleetly stomped on about twenty of the huge creatures, with one step, while a few of them scurried off into the kitchen and out of sight. The house had been in his family for as long as he could remember, and he vowed to leave once he had acquired enough money. All due to him vigorously wanting to get away from the house guest that he had grew up with.

Now as he moved silently throughout the house, he made sure not to wake anyone with his presence, while packing a few items of necessity. Just as soon as he had amassed enough items, he walked back through the different rooms, checking on his cousins, while they all lay fast asleep as if they were all waiting on Christmas morning. Once he stepped into the one room of one of his cousins that they called Dirty Diaper. You already know why they called the poor little guy Dirty Diaper, who was now practically a grown fucking man. Firstborn leaned up against the space that needed a door and mumbled out loud. "Today is the last day that this family will ever have to ask anyone for a damn thing! I'm going to make sure that I take care of each and every one of y'all. Even if it kills me." And that's exactly what was going to happen to his black ass if he fucked up Pierre Santiago's drugs and money.

He then placed a stack of hundred-dollar bills, that he had kept for himself, from the two cops that he had disposed of, on top of his mother's nightstand along with a small note. Then as he loutishly walked out of the old wood frame house, headed to his favorite hotel, so that he could embark on his new life. He gloomily turned back and stared at the blue and white painted house. "I promise that I will never have to live at this old house ever again!" He muttered. Then stepped inside of the rental, mind now focused on the hotel off of Highway Fifty-Three. The time was now around eight thirty-five in the quiet still morning as he dully pulled into the hotel parking lot, with his few amounts of clothes and thirty bricks of pure Colombian Cocaine that was about to destroy the small town. Or should I say, that he was about to destroy the small rural town with. On his face, he still adorned a sinister, evil grin as he turned the truck off and walked up the hotel door. Eager to get himself a shower and fresh start on the first day of him becoming one of North Florida's notorious Drug Dealers. The doorbell chimed with the push of his finger as he stood there waiting for the wide faced Oriental looking young man to come open the door. "Damn, these people act like they don't want to make this money!" He muttered to himself as he waited. Then suddenly appearing out of nowhere, came the young man, looking like he was half asleep. "Good morning to you sir, sorry if I woke you up," Firstborn said to the man as he cut him a half smile.

"No problem, sir, I need to be getting up anyway. I have a very busy day ahead of me!" The young man replied, now wiping the sleep from his slanted looking eyes.

"I know that's right," Firstborn mumbled.

"What was that sir?" The young man asked as he quickly turned back to face Firstborn.

"Nothing, I was just saying, I know that's right. I have a very busy day ahead of me as well."

The young man cut a wicked smile back at Firstborn, then uttered. "I see. " He then pulled out a registration form for him to fill out. "Okay sir, do you need a single room or a double room?" He asked Firstborn, who seemed to be more interested in who else might be inside of the hotel, besides the young man. Looking around as if he was thinking about robbing the place. "Sir! " The young man said as he put more bass into his voice, making sure that he got his attention.

"Oh, my bad. What was that again?"

"Would you like a single room or double room?" He asked, now sounding like he was a bit agitated.

"My fault, let me have a single room, with the room being able to connect to the room next to it."

"Fine, do you know how long you will be staying with us?"

"I don't know quite yet," Firstborn answered.

"Fine, sir. Now how will you be paying? Cash or Credit Card?" Firstborn stood still for a few seconds, then reaching into his pocket, pulling out a small clear bag. That contained a small sample of the white substance that looked like flour. The Oriental looking man looked at the bag that Firstborn had just threw up on the counter. For a moment he just stared at the bag as if he was afraid of what was inside it. Then Firstborn uttered, sounding just like a real Dope Boy.

"With this right here, my good man. That's how I'm gonna pay for it!"

The young man then swiftly scooped up the bag and inspected it. "How much is this?"

My brother's signature smile emerged onto his face as he replied. "It should be enough for me to stay here for at least a month or so!" Before he could finish his sentence, the young dope fiend was like. "Please enjoy your stay here and if I need anymore, do I come see you?"

"Certainly, my young eyed Asian friend. When you need another bump and I know you will, because no one around here has anything as pure as that what you have inside your lil' tiny ass hands."

"I see," the man replied as his face held a half smirk on it, way more different than before, now that he had enough Coke to put up his nose for a few days.

"So you know where to find me, right?" Firstborn asked as he smiled as well at the man. Knowing that he had just found his first customer of many more to come.

"Yes sir, right here at our lovely hotel. Oh, by the way sir, you're in room 113." He then swiftly threw my brother his room key and hurried him out the door, so he could get busy with his white girl.

Firstborn had just made it outside, back to the rental, when he said that he took a second to look back at the doors of the hotel where the young man had fleetly locked the doors. Once he had them secure, he dashed around the counter, swiftly taking out a small mirror, then placing the powdered substance onto the mirror. He then went into the cash register and pulled out what seemed to be a crisp hundred dollar bill. He then rolled it up and aligned up the powder for his nose. "Damn my man, you're not even going to cut that shit up, I see?" Firstborn mumbled to himself as he witnessed the man take a nice bump into his wide ass nostrils. "I knew his ass was a junkie just as soon as I heard the way his nose sounded every time he sniffed the morning stale air of the hotel. I just hope that he doesn't snort up all of that shit at one damn time," he said out loud as he drove away, headed towards room 113.

Chapter 23
Three Fuck Up!

The ride back home was exhausting, just as much as it was very tiring as I dropped off the last female. Now, I was eagerly waiting to finally get back to my humble abode. As I pulled into my driveway, I couldn't help but notice the two brand-new foreign made cars that were nicely parked in the yard. I couldn't help but smile as I walked past the two cars with my bag in my hand, saying to myself. "Wow, somebody has some real nice taste in automobiles." Then, making it into the house, I yelled out thinking that whoever the cars belonged to, just might be inside, waiting on my arrival. "Hello, is anyone here?" I then paused for a moment as I waited for someone to answer. "Oh well, now why would I think that someone would be in here? All of the girls that live here with me are still in Jacksonville." I sputtered as I ran upstairs to call my boo, Sharon. Just as I stepped into my bedroom, I found myself on my bed, taking a deep sigh, before I made the call, still having my doubts about having her and her daughter over. But there was no way that I could back out of it now, hell I had promised her ass that they could come over, so with my mind in doubt, I made the call. She must have been waiting on my phone call, since the pristine beauty answered on the first ring with. "Hello, Michael."

"Hello sexy," I replied back.

"I was sitting here asking myself. I wonder what time Michael is going to call me?"

"Oh really?"

"Yes," she replied, I could actually hear her heart racing in the background. "Yes."

"I see, well I'm calling you right now. So, are you and Bre ready for me to come pick you all up?"

"Yes, I've been waiting on your ass all day. And Bre is with my friend Maxine and her two little ones." I could actually hear her ass smiling in the background.

"Okay, well I'm on my way right now. Now you do know that I have a show tonight in Tampa, right?"

"Yes and I'm cool with that," she spat.

"Alright, well with that said, I'm on my way. "

"I can't wait," she said as we both confessed our love to one another, then hung up. Now don't get me wrong or even twisted. Like I stated before, I was a dawg. But not such a dawg that I didn't have true feelings about the ones I loved with all my heart. And I guess by now, one could see that Sharon was a big part of my heart. And there was no way that I could or would break it. So, as I ventured out to my garage, the constant thought of what I was going to do about her and her heart, pondered throughout my perplexed mind.

Meanwhile, somewhere off the shores of South Carolina, pieces of what some might have considered a jet plane had just washed up on one of the islands right outside South Carolina. At first the young man who had found a few items, didn't know what to make out of them, so he did what any young child would do. He ran home at full speed, yelling and screaming about what he had just found. Just as he reached his home, his father met him at the end of the yard, hands on hips and eyes focused on his young son.

"Father, father, look what I found!" The young man shouted. He couldn't be any older than ten, eyes bright with enthusiasm.

"What is it, son?" His father, a local business owner on the small island asked as he greeted his son.

"I don't know, but whatever it is, it seemed to have washed up on the shore," the young lad said, halfway out of breath.

"Let me see this," the child's father said as he looked at what looked like a part of a plane. His eyes wandered over the part, then he saw part of a name. Pier! was all he saw. He then bent down as he asked his son. "Was there more of this?"

"I don't know father, when I found this I ran straight home!"

"Okay son. Follow me, we have to get the boat. Then we can venture out to where more of this might be!"

***

It felt nice as hell to finally be back home, now driving my Benz over to pick Sharon up. I hadn't seen the gorgeous female since we had left for Puerto Rico. So I didn't know what to expect when I laid eyes on her for the first time in almost two weeks. So, with my sound system blasting the song, Still Waiting by my favorite artist, Prince. It had me feeling some type of way as I made a right turn onto Colonial with my windows rolled halfway down.

But just as I had made a right turn, my eyes caught something that made me think of my fool hearted brother. The time was around four fifteen in the afternoon and I still hadn't heard a damn thing from his wild and crazy ass. So without hesitation, I decided to give him a call before I was sitting in front of Sharon, due to me not wanting her to hear anything about the business he was about to start. So I dialed his number, waiting for him to answer, still asking myself. "Why in the hell hadn't this nigga called me, to let me know that he had made it back home safely?" At first I thought that maybe his black ass had got arrested for driving without a license, since he didn't have one. But hell, I didn't have one either, since at the time I had three warrants out for my arrest.

Seems as though Child Support had my license suspended and placed a warrant out for me for not paying Child Support. The other two warrants were related to my outstanding probation situation. But fuck it, if them crackers wanted my black ass, they were going to have work for that shit! There was no way in hell that I was going to turn myself in, so in other words, they were going to have to do their job and come find me.

Now back to my brother, who I don't think ever had a gotdamn Driver's License in his entire life. Then, I wondered if he still had the rental that should have been turned in already. His phone rang two times, before he answered in his baritone voice.

"Baby Boy, what's good my brother?" he said, sounding like he had a million dollars in his pockets.

"Damn lil' homie, you can't call a brother to at least let his ass know that you got home safe?" I asked him with a scowl on my face.

"My bad lil' brother, it wasn't like that. I had so much to do when I got in that the time slipped my mind."

"Alright, I can buy that one. Is everything okay?"

"Yes, my brother, everything is everything. I'm here with Twan and Fabian about to put these two hungry ass brothers to work," he said with an evil smirk smeared across his face as Twan and his kid brother sat there patiently waiting to sample his product. Both of their eyes were as large as two extra-large pizzas as they waited for their individual portions.

"I hear you brother. I guess your cousin Chai was right about you when he said that you were so smooth that you could talk a cat down from a Fish Truck!"

He started laughing as he imagined himself actually talking the cat down. "Mike, it's like this baby brother. If I tell you that it's potted eat on the Moon, you better bring soda and crackers!"

"What?" I asked, while trying not to laugh. "Nothing, Baby Boy. I'll tell you once I see you again," he said, trying to get me off the phone.

"Whatever, Firstborn, so I take it that you're still driving the rental?"

"Today is Sunday, Mike. They're closed."

"I know that James, but you could've left it at the place and dropped the keys in the slot there on the door."

"I didn't know that. I'll make sure that I turn it back in first thing in the morning. "

"Yeah, call me when you do."

"Gotcha, is there anything else, Baby Boy?"

"Yeah, please don't fuck up Pierre's money or his precious product."

"Shit, I'm 'bout to sell all this shit and make me some big money. Whenever you see my black ass again, I just might be in one of them big body Mercedes Benz, just like the one you have," he uttered, while laughing in the background.

"Whatever, James. We'll see. Just make sure you call me when you turn in that damn rental. Also, tell Twan to tell his fine ass sister, Deidra, that I said hello."

"Will do, Baby Boy, take it easy and I'll talk at cha later."

We both hung up, just as I pulled into Sharon's driveway.

Chapter 24
Mouth Wouldn't Stop Running!

I had just turned my engine off as she waltzed outside of her house, looking like the beautiful woman she was. Dressed in some nice, tight fitted acid washed shorts, along with an adorable comfortable looking shirt, that hid her cute lil' baby bump stomach.

"Hey you, it's so nice to finally see you again," I said to her with a big ass smile on my face.

"You too, handsome," she replied as she smiled back at me. She had that look in her eyes that she had the very first time we met one another. She then stood on her tippy toes as she planted a wet kiss on my lips, letting me know just how much I was truly missed. "Alright you, that's exactly how you got that lil' stomach there."

"Whatever, Michael." She voiced as she continued smiling at me. "Are you ready?"

"Yes, come inside and help me with my bags," she said as she turned, making sure I got an eye full of her nice-looking ass.

"Sure," I eagerly replied as she walked inside. "Damn, is all that yours?" She surprisingly turned around and shouted out with. "What?"

"Your ass, it's gotten bigger than before," I spoke as I stood, astonished at how fine she looked from behind.

"Whatever, Mr. Smart ass, now bring your ass on in, so we can hurry up and get back to your place," she uttered while ushering me inside her lovely home.

"Yesum, ma'am!" I replied, standing there in her doorway.

"See, your ass has all the jokes today."

"Nah, but that ass has gotten bigger than before."

"You think?" She asked.

"Yes, I know. I can't wait to hit that thing from the back," I stated as we made it inside her home.

"Whatever, see there you go," she spat.

"What? I can't want to get some of my baby mama?"

"I never said that you couldn't. But not right now. So, I'm picking up some weight?" She asked as she tried looking at her ass in the mirror, then looking over her shoulder at her ass.

"Yes, you are, and it looks really nice from where I'm standing."

"Boy, shut up!" She said. "How 'bout you grab my bags right over there in the corner."

I swiftly turned my head to see her four bags that she had sitting in the corner waiting for me. "Damn, how long you plan on staying with me?"

She smiled, then looked up at me and said, "What? If you think that those are a lot, wait until you get the ones in my room."

"Wow, hold up there, young lady, when I told you that you could come stay with me. I meant for a few days, not to move in.

"Shut up, Michael. I'm only teasing you, boy," she recited as she stood there, smile still on full display.

"Oh!"

"Now, hurry up."

Minutes later we were both headed out to my car, when she reached for the door handle. "Hold up, let me get that for you."

She paused, then eased back. "Thank you, you're such a gentleman."

"Whatever, girl. Just be careful on how you put all of that nice ass of yours down in my seat."

We were off, headed back to my place as she sat there talking a mile a minute, with one question after another one. First there was, how did I enjoy my trip and if I missed her. Her mouth was running as if it wouldn't stop, while running on and on and on, never even giving me the chance to answer not one question. The entire time that she was talking to herself, all I could do was sit there and think about the Murder Queens up in Jacksonville taking care of that one lone survivor. Then it was the constant thought of me not knowing if Rhynyia and her sister had made it back home yet. I was between a rock and a hard place at the time, now that Sharon was with me. I couldn't call Rhynyia or the Murder Queens for the fear of Sharon finding me out.

We finally made it back to my house. Sharon was still talking as I went to retrieve her bags. That's when she looked over and saw the two new automobiles off to the side of the house.

"Michael, you didn't tell me that you had purchased two new cars," she said as she stood there waiting for me to unload her things.

"I didn't, lil' Ms. Nosy as Hell. I don't even know who they belong to. They must belong to two of the girls that live here with me," I said as I wiped away the sweat from my forehead, while struggling with her heavy ass bags.

"So, wait a minute. You're telling me that you don't know who those bad ass rides belong to?"

"Nope."

"Damn, well if it's true that they belong to two of the girls here, I'm in the wrong line of work," she said with a side smirk.

"Whatever. You don't work, remember?" I said to her as I cut a side smirk back at her, then leading her into my domain.

"You got jokes," she sarcastically said behind my back. "Nah, just teasing."

"You know I'm only kidding with you, right?"

"Well, it isn't funny, Mike," she uttered as she stared at me.

"My bad, but like I said, I don't know who they belong to."

"Okay, well for real Mike, I want to dance with your group," she stated as I had just reached the foyer. For a moment there her sentiments caught me by surprise. I had to even hold my face, before turning back around to her saying, "I wish I would catch your lil' fine red ass in someone's club, shaking your hot lil' ass."

"I'm serious Mike, I want a new car too," she spoke with a serious ass unit on her face. "Girl, get that ass up the stairs. We'll talk about this later, after the club."

She then proceeded to walk upstairs. She got halfway and stopped with, "And oh, by the way, Michael. I do want to go with y'all tonight. You're not about to leave me in this big ass house by myself."

"Okay, Sharon. I hope that you have something appropriate to wear because I'm not leaving this house anymore today. I'm beat."

"You don't have to, Mister," she said as we made it to the top of the staircase. "I made sure that I brought just the right outfit for tonight," she voiced just as we both made it inside my bedroom.

"That's fine with me. You don't mind if I take a quick shower, do you?"

She was sitting on my bed by now, looking around as she looked back up at me. "Nah, go ahead!" She said as I stepped off into the bathroom. Just as I went to turn on the shower, she hit me with a question that I wasn't prepared for. "Hey, baby."

"Yeah." I shouted back from behind the bathroom door.

"Remember the night you all rescued me and Bre? "

"Yeah," I replied back. Deep down in my soul, I could sense what was about to come next. I just wasn't prepared for it.

"Well, I remember resting my head in the lap of one of your girls that I had never seen around here before, but I distinctly remember her face from somewhere. I just can't seem to remember where. What was her name and where is she at now?" She asked me, leaving me stuck, right there in my fucking bathroom. Dead in my tracks, like a deer stuck in headlights.

Ah shit, what was I going to say now? What would be my best defense? I asked myself as I swiftly tried to think of what to say to her ass. I stood frozen in time, trying to piece that night together, when it dawned on me. *Damn, I had told Yani Good to cover her face and not let her nosy ass see her face, fearing for something like this to happen.* But Sharon was smart, and I knew that she remembered seeing Yani's face on that damn picture them dead ass cops showed her ass. Things were about to fall apart for my black ass, and I couldn't think of nothing to say.

"Michael, did you hear me?" She asked as her voice became louder.

This is when I remembered what I had just told Mignon earlier in the day. Remaining calm is what I did. So, I hit Sharon back with, "Now, Sharon, you know how many females come through this group from day to day. How am I supposed to remember who she was? All I know is the female probably danced with me for one night."

"Well, in that case, Mister, we might have a problem," she said as she emerged from behind the door of my bathroom.

"Why is that?" I asked her, with a lump as big as a fucking bullfrog in my throat.

"Because I think that same female might know where my gotdamn uncle is?"

"Damn!" was all I could muster up as I turned on my shower and stood up under the hot ass water, wishing that this was all just a very bad dream.

Chapter 25
Top Speed!

Firstborn had just cut through one of the nicely packaged bricks, then took a small portion of the product out; holding up so the two young thugs could examine it more closely.

"Yeah, that's some real nice shit right there, boy," Twan uttered as his mouth watered as if he was staring at a nice, thick Pork Chop Sandwich, made from Frank's. A local town eatery nestled in the small town. Frank's had been there in Madison, Florida since I could remember. And every time that I made it back home, I would take the girls there to pick up something to eat.

"Yes sir, that's the shit! If I say so myself." Fabian added in as his eyes focused in on what Firstborn held on the tip of his finger.

"Okay, so I'm gonna start you guys off with a lil' something, so that the both of you can get your feet wet. Once you two sell all of it, come back with my money and re-up from there," Firstborn muttered, eyes and lips wanting a taste of what he had.

"Gotcha! So how much do we start off with?" Twan asked, while rubbing his two hands together as if his ass had just hit the Lotto.

"Here, you two take this brick, break it down between the both of you and then, we go from there," Firstborn recited, just like a real-life Dope Boy, who was trying to make a come up.

"Okay and what's the price on the Birds, you know, in case we run into some real big playas out there in these streets?" Fabian asked from the back seat. "Shiiit let's say, round about thirty-five a key. Whatever you two make off the side, it's all yours. Just make sure that I get mine."

"What? So you're selling these things for the low-low my nigga! They usually go for at least forty-five a key!" Fabian yelled as he slid his ass up in the seat.

Firstborn then cohesively turned his head in the direction of his young protege, smiling as he announced. "I know this, man. My young-minded friend, that's why you sell a whole bird for whatever price you like, you two just make sure you get me what's owed back to me."

"Nigga, that's what's up! Fuck splitting that shit up! Give me four of them thangs right muthafucking now! I have at least two niggas I can get these off to right this minute!" Fabian shouted, all while Twan couldn't believe the good luck that had just found their ass.

"You sure?" Firstborn asked as he turned to look at the young man.

"Hell yeah. I'm sure. Twan tell this fool," Fabian shouted, all excited and shit.

"He ain't lying Smooth. We both have a few brothers up in Tallahassee who be needing that work, so if you can trust us with a few Birds on consignment, we should have you your money in no time," Twan voiced as his face held a serious unit.

"Well hell, fuck splitting this shit up. Why don't I just give you niggas ten bricks, five a piece. And you two do you."

The pair looked at one another, then back at Firstborn before uttering. "That's what's up my nigga, do the damn thing then!"

Firstborn then went up under the seat, pulling out ten nicely wrapped packages of Cocaine. "So this is what you two want, right?" Their eyes couldn't focus on what they were now gazing at, but their mouths were just a step ahead of them.

"Hell yeah, man, give me them thangs!" Twan barked.

"Here you go. Alright now, remember this is a man's game now, so please don't play with it! Stay your ass on the porch if you're not ready for this shit!" Firstborn uttered with a very stern looking face.

"Gotcha!" The brothers said in unison, eager to step out there in the world. "Here, put them in this bag and call me just as soon as you two get off of them."

"No problem. Thanks, and look for us to call you back in a few days."

"Alright you two, the man that I got the work from don't play about his money or his work. So that means neither me," Firstborn said while rubbing his two hands together.

"We hear you man." Twan shouted. "Cool, now y'all two haul ass while I go find my nigga so he can cook this shit up for me."

"Yeah, holla at cha nigga. Peace," The brothers both said as they jumped out of the truck, swiftly running back inside the house. After watching the two run back into the house, he placed the truck in reverse and was trying to back out of their driveway, when he heard someone calling him by his nickname whenever he resided in the small town.

"Smooth, yo' Smooth! Hold up! Wait a minute." The very bright skinned with hazel brown eyes yelled out to him, while running at top speed, trying to get to his truck.

The very attractive looking female was damn near out of breath as she stepped up to the driver side of the vehicle. Smiling, showing off her pearly white teeth as she said.

"So, you're gonna just come over here and leave without speaking to me, huh?" His face held a slight smile as he stared back at the young lady.

"Nah, I didn't even know that you were home. What's up, beautiful?"

"Whatever, Smooth. What's up with you? And where is your handsome ass baby brother at?" Deidra asked as she stood to catch her breath, while placing her hands on her superb looking waist.

"I guess somewhere back in Orlando. I just got off the phone with his ass a few minutes ago," he said, eyes roaming the curvaceous body of the young female.

"Well, the next time that you speak to him, tell his ass that I said hello and to call me."

"Will do, Baby Girl, now let me get out of here. I have a lot of work to get to," he spoke, mind set on one thing and one thing only. "I see, I ran past my brothers with smiles over their faces as if they had just hit a big payday," she said, then came back with. "What in the hell did you give them two fools?"

"Ahhhh, nothing really. Just some weight that they claim they can get off for a nigga." Her praline eyes were about to pop out of her head when he uttered the words some weight.

"For real?" She asked, excited as a small kid on Christmas morning.

"Yep," he replied, now opening up the door in which she had already fell into, face first.

"Can a sister have a taste, so I can see just how good that shit is? " She asked as her face now looked as if she was about to cry.

My brother looked back at her, feeling sorry for the dear girl, then saying, "Listen, Dee. I really don't want to get you hooked on this stuff, girl. This here is the real deal. You see this is the purest shit that you have ever seen." He then pulled out a small bag of the white powdered substance, that caused her lovely looking hazel brown eyes to enlarge when she witnessed the Yayo. She quickly tried to snatch the bag from his clenched hand as he shouted. "Hey girl, stop playing!" As he yanked the bag back from her hand. She then began to plead and beg for just a small sample. "C'mon Smooth, just let me have a small taste, please?"

"Damn, girl, get in!" He yelled as he knew what was about to happen next. With that said, she quickly ran around to the passenger door, then jumped in.

"So, what do I have to do to get me a nice taste of some of that good shit from down south?" Her face held a wide smile on it as she sat there, infatuated with the product there before her.

"Nothing, girl, just chill. I'm taking you back to my hotel room. We can decide what you can do for me once we get back there. Besides, I have to finish packing up the product," he said to her as he watched her place her seat belt around her firm, tight waist.

Once she had it in place, she laid her head back against the headrest and said, "That's fine with me. Hell, I wasn't doing anything any damn way."

"I hear you," he replied as he put the truck in reverse, then slowly backed out of her driveway.

Just as he placed the truck in drive, she looked over at my brother and asked him, "Hey, Smooth. Does your brother still have that group of girls? What was the name of the group again?"

"Yes, he does. You know he's always going to have them around him, all the way up until the day he dies. And the group's name is the Florida Hot Girls," he muttered as he sped down the road, headed back to his hotel.

Chapter 26
Butt Ass Naked!

Apollo South was a little bit different than before, when the ladies and I stepped inside. It seemed as though the Club had stepped up its game when it came to hiring the right type of females to dance inside their club now. Just as soon as my ladies walked inside of the club, you could feel the vibe that everyone had, once the Florida Hot Girls had entered the building, located off of 40th Street. I had my usual crew of elegant looking women, while Richard had a few of the new chicks with him. As soon as DJ Don Juan witnessed the ladies and I walk through the door, he went wild over the speaker system.

"Oh shit! Ladies and Gentlemen, may I have your attention please. The world-famous Florida Hot Girls have just stepped off into the building, so please get your money right and let's make it thunderstorm up in this bitch, on every single one of them bad ass females!" This is when the ladies all began to sway their hips from side to side as all eyes fixed on them, strutting their way into the club and into some of the patrons' pockets.

"So, I take it he's talking about your girls, correct?"

I gazed down at her, still somewhat bitter about her and the fact that she might know who Yani was. "You better believe it, sweetheart." Just as soon as I uttered those sentiments, there came that funny feeling again. That feeling as if I knew I was the shit for having a group of beautiful, exotic looking women by my side.

So, while ushering Ms. Lady to my table in the back of the club, my ladies stood watching the ladies that were already performing on the crowded dance floor. Talking amongst one another, while waiting for me to give them the signal to go ahead and get dressed. When Sharon saw that I had stopped at the table, she quickly asked. "Right here?"

"Yeah, right here, beautiful," I said as she sat down on her newly found Goldmine.

But before I could even get my night started, you know who walked over to my table and asked, "Mike, what's up? Can we go ahead and dress in?"

"Yeah, I guess you guys still have a dressing room, Chyna!" I shouted, since the music was blazing from the speakers. Deep down, I was praying that they still had a dressing room since they hadn't danced there in a while. But that thought was quickly banished from my head when the house girl motioned for them to go ahead to their usual dressing room. Once the last female dashed off towards the dressing room, I was back to work, just as if I hadn't missed a beat. "Excuse me, Sharon, I'll be right back."

She pulled at my silk Versace shirt, asking me, "Hold up, baby, where are you going?"

"Give me a minute. I have to give the ladies some instructions."

"For real? So, you're going to just leave all this right here, all by myself?" She asked as she ran her hands over her body. I guess she wanted me to see just how fine she was.

"Yep, and if all of that is gone by the time I get back, it only means that all of that wasn't mine in the first place!" I said to her as I hurried away, laughing to myself.

"Whatever, Mister Smart Ass!" She shouted as I could hear laughing as I continued walking away, trying my best to get to my precious stable of adorable women.

When I got to the door, I didn't even knock, I just walked straight through the door, staring at nothing but butt naked ass and shaved vaginas. Boy, what a pretty sight to witness.

"Alright, ladies, y'all know what to do, you have about twenty minutes to get that ass ready, before I need to see you ladies out there getting that muthafucking bread!"

"Whatever, Mike! Your black ass just wanted to see our kitty cats! We know what to do, Mister!" Chyna yelled as she walked right past me, butt ass naked...

She knew she had me rocked up, just as her gorgeous ass waltzed right by me. "See, why you teasing me with that lil' ass pussy, staring directly at me?" I spat.

She turned on her heels and said, "Nigga, you know your black ass wanted to see this pussy anyway. That's why you're back here. You need to be back outside that door, with that lil' chick that looks a lot like Sexy Redd." She then smiled at me as she pretended to drop something on the floor, then slowly bending over, so I could see how her pussy looked from the back, spread eagle.

"Dammmnnn! I guess she told your ass, Mike! And she's right, your new girl, looks just like Sexy Redd," Suga Bear shouted as I just stood there, speechless.

"I know that's right," Chyna said as she stood back, then placing her index finger and thumb on her pussy lips, then spreading them apart, so that I could see her lil' Man In The Boat. At that moment, I was once again stuck.

"Yeah, she does look like Sexy Redd, doesn't she? So what, that still doesn't mean for you girls to be in here worrying about lil' ol' me. Now get dressed and make my money! I need my money!" I shouted as I clapped my hands together, just like Morris Day did in the movie, *Purple Rain*. Just as I reached the door, I had to turn around and say. "And oh, by the way, fuck you Chyna!"

"Whatever, Mike. You wish you could fuck all of this good ass pussy!" She shouted at the back of my head as I made a dash for the door, before John Boy and I wanted some of what my eyes were seeing.

Moments later, I was back at my table with Sharon, still having that surprised look on my face. She must have sensed something was wrong with me as she placed her soft hands on my wrist and asked me. "Hey, you okay?"

"Yeah, just a lil' thirsty that's all."

"Do you need me to grab you something to drink, real quick?"

"Nah, I'm good. I'll get something just as soon as the ladies step out of the dressing room."

"So, this is what you do when you come down here on Sunday nights?"

"Yes ma'am, this is how I make my money on Sundays."

"Must be nice to sit here and watch butt naked hoes all night!" She said with a bit of sarcasm in her mild voice.

"Excuse me, what was that?" I asked, head bent down so that I could really hear what she was saying.

"Nothing. I wonder how it is when you go out of town for the weekend and leave me home all by myself?" She asked me as she looked around the club, surveying her surroundings. I was tentatively listening as I sat there staring at my big-headed ass cousin, Richard. He was over in the darkness of the club, rolling himself another blunt.

"It's okay, just a lil' different vibe when we go out of town," I replied, while shaking my head at what Richard was doing. Since he was already high, from smoking all the way down to Tampa. I couldn't hold my composure any longer as I abruptly turned to him and said, "Boy, you just done turned into a full out junkie, I see!"

He cut a half smirk at me as he fell off of the bar stool, then asked me, "Why you say that cuz? I'm good. I just look high, that's all."

"Yeah right, Richard. Man, your ass is higher than a fucking kite right about now!"

"Mike, baby let him have his fun!" Sharon cut in and said in his defense. "If the poor man wants to smoke and get high, let him get high. You know he just lost his baby mama a few weeks ago!"

"I know, but who's going to watch the crew of ladies that he has with him? If he's all high and shit?" I angrily replied as I looked up to see fine ass Chyna walking our way. "Excuse me Mike, Don Juan wants to speak with you inside the DJ Booth."

"Alright, thank you Chyna." After I acknowledged her, she turned on away, sashaying her small ass hips, making sure that I noticed that she had on an outfit that had her ass cheeks on full display. If you would have asked me, it looked like the damn outfit that Prince wore on stage one night on television. I mean both of her lil' small, red ass cheeks were cut right out of her outfit.

What broke my attention on her fine ass was Sharon's voice, saying, "She's cute, Michael. What's her name again?"

"Chyna, Sharon. Give me a quick minute while I see what the DJ wants."

"No problem bae, just hurry back before these niggas start coming over here trying to holla at me."

This is when I reached over and planted a kiss on her soft lips, then whispered in her ear with, "Nah, you good, remember. You have weed head ass Richard here to watch over you. You were the one who said let the man smoke, right?"

"Whatever, Mike. With the way his ass is swaying back and forth on that stool, his ass can barely watch himself," she said.

It actually made me laugh. "See, I told your ass! Now, how do you think I feel about my gotdamn dancers?" I shouted as I scurried away, trying to see what in the hell Don Juan wanted.

Chapter 27
Wearing That Ass!

I had just walked past the bar area when I heard all the commotion as the rest of my lovely team of women walked out of the dressing room, looking ravishing as usual. Right then I realized that I hadn't heard from Mignon nor the other girls. So quickly thinking, I shouted over for Chyna, not knowing what she might say when I asked her.

"Hey, Chyna." Her lips were curled up as she dully approached me.

"Yes, Mike. You know you're holding me up from getting my bread, right?" She asked me, lips now really curled up.

"Yes girl, I know. But this is really important."

"Okay, what?" she asked, now with both hands on those nice hips of hers.

"I'm going to need for you to watch over the ladies until Mignon gets here."

She stopped with the look of annoyance on her face. She even looked around the club before saying, "Wait a minute, where is your precious Mignon and the rest of them females at?"

"Not now, Chyna, please."

"What?" She asked as she stood there with her mouth wide open.

"Chyna please, all I'm asking you to do, is just step in and be the manager until she gets here."

"Wait a minute Mister, when I wanted to be a gotdamn manager, your lil' boo thang told me that there wasn't any room for me as a manager!" She said with attitude.

"Okay and now I'm telling your fine red ass to step in and be a manager for just a few hours. Is that a problem? If so, I'll ask Lil' Kitty?" Her head turned to gaze over at Lil' Kitty, then back at me.

"Nah, with the way her poor eye is looking, she's not going to be able to handle that daunting task tonight, or any other night for a few days."

"Funny, Chyna."

"For real! You see how her ass is over there looking, standing up there on that damn speaker."

"Yes, I seen it already. So what, you're going to do it?"

"Yeah, I guess so. So this means that I don't have to pay your tip out fee if I do this favor for you, do I?" She asked as her face revealed a beautiful smile.

"You're really asking a lot here, Chyna?"

"What, C'mon Mike. I let you see all of this pussy earlier and you're acting like this?"

I smiled back at her as I thought back to how pretty her small ass pussy looked, then said.

"Fuck that! When are you going to let me sample some of that nice looking pussy of yours?" Her face was still holding onto that bright smile of hers.

"Ahhhhh, let me think about it," she said, then turned her head and was just about to walk away, when she swiftly turned back around and said, "Nope!"

"That's so fucked up!" I replied, sounding all dejected and disgusted. For a minute there, I actually thought that she was about to give in to my begging ass.

"I know, now go see what Don Juan wants, so I can get back to my customer, who's doing something that you never do."

I reached out for her arm, then pulled her back into me. "And what's that?"

"Pay Michael. He's paying me to see all of this! Now bye!
"She then snatched her arm away, leaving me there alone to
my thoughts. A few minutes later, I was on my way over to
the DJ Booth, where Don Juan was eagerly waiting. Just as
soon as I hit the door of the Booth, his face lit up, with him
yelling. "Yo, Mike, what's good my man?"

"Nothing much playa, how has life been treating you?" I
asked him as we both gave each other a light fist bump.

"Man, I'm good, what about you?"

"I'm good, now that I'm back in Tampa."

"I hear you. But what I want to know is who is that lil'
fine red thang that came in the door with you tonight?" I
acted surprised and then shouted. "Oh, talking about the lil'
shortie back there at the table?" Trying to act as if I didn't
already know that he was checking for my girl.

"Yes sir, my nigga. Is she dancing tonight?" I broke his
heart when I answered. "Her name is Sharon and no she's not
my brother. She's not here tonight or no other night." His
face changed as he grayly asked me. "Why, what's up with
that?"

"That one there, is something on a more personal level
my friend."

He then figured it out, when he came back at me with.
"Oh, I see. So in other words, you're fucking that one?"

"Indeed my young brother. You could say that I'm
wearing that fine, red ass the fuck out!"

His tongue and words became slurred as he asked me.
"Whhhhaaaat, abouttt Sexy Reddddd? Where is she at?"

"She had to go back to Puerto Rico for her brother's
funeral. We buried him yesterday, so I'm really just getting
back into town."

"Sorry to hear that."

"Yeah, me too. Like I said, we all flew back into town
right after the funeral. First we stopped off in Duval, then we
came down here tonight, to show our love to Club Apollo."

"Boy, you sure do a lot of traveling."

"Yes sir, that's what we do," I replied with a devilish grin on my face. Not even realizing that Sexy Redd still hadn't got in touch with me. "I see, so when the cat's away, the mouse will play."

"Something like that young playa," I replied as the young brother then said something that caused me to halt, right there in my tracks. "You know, just by glancing at your lil' shortie real quick from a distance, she kind of looks like her and Sexy Redd could be sisters."

"For real?" I replied as I thought back to her mother wanting to drop the news on my ass. My mind went a drift for a moment, until I heard him say. "One thing that I can honestly say about you Mike, is that you always keep you something nice and fine on your arm."

"Yes sir. That's why we call it Arm Candy, my young brother." Just as soon as I uttered those sentiments, the woman of the hour walked into the DJ Booth, with Richard walking right behind her, throwing his hands up in the air as if he was trying to say. My bad cousin, I tried to stop her! I was mean mugging his crazy ass, all while Sharon was looking up at me, screaming. "So you just going to leave me sitting at the table all by myself while you're over here running your mouth?" I quickly turned my attention to her, then yelled. "Yo, Don Juan, it was nice talking to you bro, but I have to get back to more important things right now!"

"Peace Mike." He shouted as he stared at how nice her ass looked, while she walked behind me, still yelling. "Did you forget that I was even here with you tonight, Michael?"

"Nah, bae. He started talking to me about you and one thing led to another, please forgive me. I promise that it won't ever happen again," I said as I had walked past the opening of the DJ Booth, but stopped when I heard the DJ playing some new track that was taking off at the moment.

The song had a nice vibe to it, as the female kept saying, *"My neck, my back!"*

"Hold up, Sharon, let me ask him something real quick?" I said to her as I stopped in my tracks, then turned to a smiling Don Juan. "Yo, Don Juan, who is that on the track?"

"You like that shit, don't cha?" He asked, wide ass smile all over his face.

"Hell yeah!" I replied as I stood there, bouncing to the beat of the nice sounding track.

"Her name is Kyia and the name of the song is *My Neck, My Back.* She's a new artist that's taking over the city. And get this, she wants me to be her DJ." He screamed, still overly excited.

"You don't say?" I replied as I turned to walk away with Sharon in two, both of us headed to the dance floor area. This is where we both stood, observing a few of my ladies doing their thing, then thinking to myself, *This will be my very last night that I ever bring your ass out to a club with me!* Not just because of what had just happened, but for the simple reason of me not being able to work the club if she was right there by my side. A rule that I would have to follow for the next couple of years, if I wanted to remain on top of my game.

Now while standing there pondering over my thoughts and dancing to the song that would eventually be a hit single, Sharon had her fine, thick ass gyrating on my stiff dick as she admired Chyna and Charlie B dancing on stage. I was just about to get into her movement on me, when I looked over to the right of the stage, to catch Lil' Kitty still dancing on top of one of the club speakers. That's when I yelled out to her lil' thin ass, "Alright now, don't come crying to me when your lil' narrow ass falls off of that damn speaker and breaks your lil' ass neck!"

She cut an evil stare back at me, with that one eye sticking out like a sore thumb. "Whatever, Mike! And if I do, you better be right there to catch my lil' thin ass!"

"Yeah, right!" I shouted back at her as I looked back over to the left of the club, to see Peekachu walking her light skinned ass into the DJ Booth, with that same two-dollar thong on, engrossed up her red ass.

"Hey, Mike, isn't that the one female that they call Peekachu?" Sharon asked, while sounding all excited and shit. All because she saw Peekachu. Hell, she wasn't a star yet, so I don't know why she was so excited? I guess it was the thrill and all for being there amongst the girls that night.

"Yes, that's the one who calls herself Peekachu. Why?"

"Oh nothing. It's just that earlier tonight, I overheard her tell one of the other girls that she was trying to make enough money to buy herself a nice car."

"Oh yeah?"

"Yes. See, she has the same thing on her mind as I do." I then placed my arms around her waist, then leaned down into her ear with.

"I hear you Sharon and like I said I will talk to you about that later. And besides, I don't know why Peekachu is trying to buy a car. Hell, she doesn't even have a fucking Driver's License!"

"For real?" Sharon asked, as if she was surprised and shit.

"Yes, for real." She then turned her head towards the door and pointed at the females walking through the front door, looking just like some professional dancers in their street clothes.

"Mike, look!" My head swiftly snapped towards the door, to witness the cutest sight I ever wanted to see. Because walking through the front door, was none other than some bad ass females, who all had on some fucking sunglasses in the dark of the night. My night had just got better when I looked to see Mignon, Tameia, Nicole, Entyce, Strawberry and of course my girl, bad ass Mo Money, waltzing through the open door. As if they were about to take over the small club on 40th street. Tampa, Florida and Apollo South, were about to be turned out by them females who you couldn't help but love. They were the infamous Murder Queens. And there I was, nestled up with one who just might have been a

Murder Queen herself. I just didn't know it at the time. All I could do was shake my head from side to side as I stood there, face holding a smile, while my heart beat fast and hard, just standing there staring at those girls who I couldn't help but love.

Chapter 28
Act Up!

I was so damn happy to see my girls that I believe I actually had a lone tear that had escaped from my right eye. The rest of my tears I refused to let escape, there was no way that I was going to let the people in that club see me cry. Like I said earlier, the club was about to take off, especially when Don Juan saw them walking through the door, searching the club for me. He must have been feeling the same way as I was, due to him cranking up the sound system. "Okay everybody, that was my girl, Kyia, singing her new hit Can Wing With It Now throw your hands up and do like my man, Orlando Mike always says and Break Bread! Break muthafucking Bread! They're here y'all! The rest of them bad ass bitches, who we all know, as the muthafucking Florida Hot Girls!" He then put on the song Where Da Cash At? by the Currency and lil' Wayne, featuring Remy Ma. The club began to go wild as all the ladies went to swinging their arms wildly, asking all the men the one question, "Where Da Cash At?"

The song and the beat even had my lil' boo, throwing her hands up in the air, singing right along with Remy Ma. "Now what do you know about this song?" I asked.

She turned around with a giant smile across her face and said, "Whatever, my nigga. Where da cash at?"

I couldn't do nothing but look at her ass, smiling as well and said, "Right where it's supposed to be. Inside my fucking pockets! "We both started laughing as the crowded club continued singing along with the song.

Meanwhile, over at the entrance of the club, Mo Money was right up under Nicole, looking for myself, when she asked her. "Where in the hell is our boo at?" Nicole already knew where I was, due to her spotting Sharon and I, standing over by the dance floor as soon as they all walked in. Our eyes had locked in on one another as soon as she hit the entrance, I guess you can say that we had that certain chemistry between one another. It's funny, since Nicole and I, had only knew one another for just a few months, but still had some type of connection between one another.

"Now listen, Mo Money. Before I point out where he is, you have to promise me that you're going to remain calm and not act out?"

"What?" Mo Money asked as she stared at Nicole.

"Mo Money, you already know how I know how you act about the man."

"Yeah, but why? Is his ass somewhere fucking one of the new chicks already?"

"No silly, his ass is right over there, hugged up with the female he was on the phone with this morning," Nicole said as she pointed in my direction.

"Oh, so that's his lil' boo thang, huh?" She asked, lips curled up.

"Something like that, Mo Money. Now remember, you said that your cool."

"I am."

"Okay, so don't you go and do anything stupid."

"I'm not. She's cute, but not as cute as we are," she mumbled to Nicole, both of their eyes still glued on me and Sharon.

"At least his black ass has some fucking taste," Mo Money finished saying as I could feel her eyes staring directly at my forehead.

"Okay Mo Money, you said that you would be nice," Nicole uttered, cutting her eyes over at me, then giving me a quick wink of the eye. "I am Nicole, I'm just admiring his taste in women, that's all," she recited with a slight bit of jealousy laced in her voice.

"Excuse me Sharon, let me go holla at my other girls real quick." I quickly darted off before she could protest. When I stepped up to Chazz and Suga Bear along the wall of the club, drinking and smoking with some local thugs, my eyes couldn't help but stare at the pair as my mouth spit out something smart and witty, directed at the both of them. "Boy, you two sure know how to pick 'em, don't cha?"

"You damn right, Pimp and we already have our fucking Tip Out Fee! So just pretend that your black ass is Michael Jackson and Just Beat It!"

"Very fucking funny, Suga Bear!" I yelled as I continued walking towards the ladies at the door of the club.

Just as I stepped in front of the ladies, I greeted them with, "Glad you ladies finally decided to join us!" Their faces all held smiles, all except Mo Money.

Mignon cut in with, "Your ass better be glad that we all decided to come. Hell, that was a long ass drive, from Jacksonville to Orlando, then Tampa."

"You're right. Now y'all see how that shit feels! I do it all the time, while you ladies are busy sleeping the entire way."

"Whatever. Where is the dressing room so we can get dressed in and get this paper?"

"Damn, Mo Money, who pissed on your neck and told you that it was raining?"

"No one, it's just the simple fact that I see you over there all hugged up with your lil' boo thang, pretending that you don't see me and Nicole standing right in front of your black ass!" Mo Money growled as I stood there not knowing if I was embarrassed or just made shame.

"Well damn, are you fucking serious?" I asked with a disgusted look on my face. Before Mo Money could even muster up an answer, Mignon stepped in with her two cents.

"Hey Mike, listen. You and ole girl can do that shit on y'all's time; we didn't come here to hear that shit! Now can we go dress in, please?"

I could see that she was about to get hot. So I answered her back with, "Why of course ladies, please be my guest." They were just about to walk away, when I snatched the living hell out of young ass Mo Money's arm. "Listen here, young lady! Stop with the jealous act. I told your ass what time it was. Now stop acting like your damn shoe size and act your damn age. Once I get rid of her, all of me is yours, do you understand?"

"But Mike..." She tried to say as I looked directly into those pretty eyes of hers.

"But my ass! Stop it! Like I said, when she's gone, it's all yours! Now do we have an understanding?" Her head hung low as she took her fingers and pulled a fake smile onto her lovely face.

"Yes Mike," she answered with a lone tear in her right eye as Nicole came back and took her by her arm and whispered.

"You promised me that you wouldn't act up, now let's go." As they walked away, I could have sworn that I heard the little heifer say. "You better hurry up and get rid of her red ass before I do!" Now that is where I should have checked her young ass, but I was too far gone with all the attention the rest of the girls were receiving at the time to pay any attention to her threats. This was when I casually turned to witness the ladies walking off headed towards the dressing room, when Chyna walked down off stage.

"So now that your precious other females are here, there is no need for me to pretend that I'm not, right?" At that moment, I had to put on a fake smile, due to me still being perturbed with Mo Money.

"Yeah, thanks a lot, Chyna."

"No problem, boss," she uttered with a smile.

"Alright Chyna, I told your ass about that smart ass mouth of yours!"

Her head quickly turned to look back at me. "What? You are the boss, correct?"

"Not now Chyna, go ahead and get back to your many clients," I voiced, while walking away, heading back over to where Sharon stood. Moments later, I was a few feet away from Sharon, when I caught Candy, Tarshay, rolling herself up a nice thick blunt, with block headed ass Richard, standing beside her, waiting to put his dried crusted ass lips on it. I just shook my head from side to side, while standing there searching the club for the rest of my team.

As I stood there patiently waiting to see all of them, dancing throughout the club, I spotted Carmen and JK standing over by the men's restroom, talking to one another about leaving the club with one of the Wide Receivers from the Tampa Bay Bucs football team. They told me later that he was running around the club, flashing nothing but Big Faces at all of my team of women. Five minutes later, your boy Richard was standing beside Sharon and I, frantically coughing and trying to speak to me at the same damn time. Beating on his chest, like he was an African drum at ceremonial time, with saliva and what looked like snot, running down his nose. The man looked a hot mess as he gathered himself together and asked me.

"Hey Mike, have you seen the rest of my girls?" He could barely stand up straight after he had been coughing and choking for about two minutes, nonstop.

"Nah Rich, I haven't seen any of your girls, come to think about it, I can't remember the last time I seen them at all tonight," I replied, while making sure none of his saliva or snot, got on my silk shirt. Forget the fact that we were cousins, I don't care who his ass was, he wasn't getting any of that shit on me.

"Damn, I turn my head for five minutes and somehow they all disappear."

"I don't think they disappeared Richard, I think half of them are in the dressing room."

"Thanks, Sharon," he said as he hurried over to the dressing room so that he could collect their tip out fee.

He had got at least a few steps away, when I bent over and asked, "Damn, Sharon. How did you know that half of his team of women were inside of the dressing room?"

She dully turned to me. "Due to all the things that I have been through in the last few days, Michael. It has caused me to pay very close attention to my immediate surroundings." Just as the words had rolled off of her luscious looking lips, it was as if a light had went off inside of my head.

"Sharon, do you know that lawyer you're going to hire to represent you in your lawsuit against the police department?"

"No, not yet. Why do you ask?"

"Because, that's where you're going to get the money from so that you can purchase that new car." A giant smile magically appeared on her face as she replied in excitement. "You're absolutely right, I had forgotten all about that. I guess you do think of more than just the Florida Hot Girls!"

I then gave her my boyish smile as I leaned back up against the wall, gazing at Nicole and Mo Money, who were now dancing with one another on the stage in front of us. With about twenty guys around the stage, making it thunderstorm at their feet.

Chapter 29
The Back Bone!

While standing there, mesmerized at how the both of them were carrying on, up on stage, I caught Strawberry out the corner of my eye, walking our way. She had just got a few inches away as she lightly tapped Sharon on her shoulder and muttered. "Excuse me pretty lady, can I speak with Mike for a moment please?"

"No problem Strawberry, just make sure you don't keep him tied up all night long."

"No problem, Sharon, I'll have his ass back to you before you know it." Strawberry and I then walked to the back of the club. With me gazing at the back of her head, mumbling. "This better be good, Strawberry."

"Trust me, it is," she uttered as she stopped and then turned to look at me. She then took her time and articulated how Marquise had departed this earth. I was standing, halfway facing her, with part of my body still looking towards the stage, still keeping my eye on Sharon and my two special females dancing on stage.

"So, are you all sure that his ass is dead this time?"

"Yes, Mike. I made sure of that! If his black ass lives through all of those bullets that we put in his ugly ass, they might want to change his name to Superman."

My face held a smirk as I asked her. "Okay, so everything should be good, is there anything else?"

"Yes, one more thing," she uttered as her head hung low.

"What is it now?"

147

"You know Entyce is leaving the group right?"

"Yes, she mentioned something to me earlier about her wanting to leave."

"Okay, well you might want to speak with your two favorite girls, then."

"What two?" I asked for the fear of finding out what two she was talking about.

Then she hit me with, "Mignon and Nicole."

I was just about to walk away, when she said their names. This caused my ass to abruptly stop and turn back to her with a dumbfounded look on my face. "Why?" I asked.

She just shrugged and said, "I don't know, you have to ask them. I guess they will tell you once we all get back home." That was all she said as she walked away, leaving me alone to myself.

As I stood there in the back of that club that night, it was as if I was the only one there, when she recited those awful words to me. What was I going to do without the backbone of the group with me? I asked myself, standing there as if I had just lost my best friend.

Strawberry had just walked past Sharon, as she went to join the girls on stage. When Sharon must have stopped her. "Hey you, where is my boo?"

"Oh, I left him at the back of the club. He should still be back there." She pointed in my direction as Sharon replied.

"Okay, I see him," she said as she began walking my way. She must have sensed that something was amiss, because she got over to me in mere seconds, placing her hand softly on my shoulder and then asking me.

"Michael, is there something wrong? Why are you standing back here all alone in the dark, looking as if you have lost your best friend?"

I drowsily lifted my head up and stared directly in her eyes. "I have. I just found out that I'm about to lose the backbone of the group!" I stood there, refusing to let my tears escape from my eyes as my hot tears began to well up in the bottom of them. One thing for sure and two things for certain, was that whenever Michael Vallentino lost one female, he would always gain two. And if he lost two, his black ass was going to gain four more in their place. At that time and moment, who was I fooling, if they were leaving, there was no way that I was about to just sit back and let my group crumble. Hell to the nah.

***

I woke up that Monday morning with that ghastly, awful feeling that something unpleasant was about to happen to me. You know that uncanny feeling that you're about to have a very bad day? But what was even more puzzling to me, was the simple fact that I just don't know what it was that I feared. It was kind of like the same exact feeling I had, when them FEDs came arresting me that night inside of Club Pony, in Jacksonville, some years later.

It was a feeling like you knew something was about to happen, almost like you could see into the future. I wish I could have, then maybe I wouldn't have ended up where I am today. This dreadful feeling that I had acquired during my tenacious and very stressful military career, that somehow followed me back into the civilian world. So I laid there in my bed, tossing and turning, not wanting to muster up any strength so that I could handle any of my daily activities. My mind went a drift, from situation to situation, while all I wanted to do was just lay there in bed, hoping and praying that my feelings wouldn't get the best of me. And now that I think about it. That day, actually felt just like it feels when you wake up and find out it's raining outside. Yeah, that's it. Just like a rainy day, which puts you in the mood of not wanting to get up. In which on this particular day, I didn't want to get up, not if what was about to happen to me was already known.

Sharon had woke up around nine a.m. so that she could get her daughter off to daycare, leaving me all alone to ponder over my daily affairs. 'Okay Mike, pull yourself together my friend. The day isn't going to stop because you want it to.' I mumbled to myself as I sluggishly walked over to my sound system. After I hit play, the song that resonated through my speakers was the song by the group, Troop and the song was titled, Sweet November. It was the perfect song for my somber feeling. Now with the song playing, I sluggishly walked over to my walk-in closet in search of something to wear.

After choosing my attire for that day, I walked back out into my bedroom to hear someone lightly tapping at my door. Thinking that it was Nicole knocking, wanting to release some morning tension. A devilish smile appeared on my face as I hurried to the door. Hell, I needed to release some tension myself. But when I opened it, there standing behind the door were the two who I hadn't expected to see that early. Both of them were fully clothed as they stood there, faces holding a look of glum.

"Excuse me Mike, can we both have a few minutes of your time please?" Mignon asked as they both stood there. Somber looks on their faces made it clear of what was on their minds.

"Sure, come on in," I said to her as Nicole softly walked in behind her, with her head held down as if she was looking for something on the floor. She had that look as if she had dropped some money on the floor and had forgotten to pick it up. As they both walked into my room, I stood at the door, saying to myself. 'Well, I guess I won't be fucking Nicole, this morning.' The both of them took a seat on my bed as I waltzed over to them, noticing something very different about Nicole's appearance. I immediately thought back to the night when I had got back in from Puerto Rico. I noticed it then, but Mignon suggested that Nicole keep silent that night. But now that I was witnessing her flat stomach again, I was a bit curious as to what was the problem?

"Hold on, before you two start on me. Nicole, is there something that you want to tell me?" She looked over at Mignon, then back at me as Mignon nodded her head up and down in approval of answering my question to her.

"Go ahead Nicole, it's okay."

Nicole then cleared her semi parched throat as she looked up at me with tears slowly snaking down her gorgeous face. "Yes Michael, I have been wanting to tell you this since you arrived back from your trip."

"What is it? Is it about the baby?" I asked. I just had to know.

Then, she replied back with, "I guess now is a better time than ever."

This is when I braced my heart and feelings for the worst. "Okay Nicole, you have my full attention and I'm all ears," I replied as I walked over to the window, not wanting to see her face, nor wanting them to see me shed a few tears of my own. Just as I made it over to the window, the song by the group LeVert, Quiet Storm, came slowly playing through my speakers. The song even had the sounds of rain falling in the background. It had to be the perfect song for that moment, since she had tears, I had tears, even Mignon had fucking tears coming down.

Then Nicole's voice cut through the song with, "I don't know how to start," she choked up.

"Just start with the beginning," I uttered, hands behind my back. I was standing tall, but I was just about to be weak at the knees, when I heard her blurt out, "I lost the baby!" My girl cracked as she burst into an awful bout of tears and sadness. Her words hit my ass like a ton of bricks, causing me to feel like I had just been punched by Mike Tyson in my stomach.

Don't get me wrong, it would have been very difficult for me to adjust to three females having my child at the same time. But Yahweh knows, I didn't want to lose the child I was about to have with her.

It took me a few moments as I stood there stunned, then I fell to my knees, placing my hand on her thigh and asking her. "How, what happened?"

"The night that everything went South!" She said as she began to cry, hysterically and me trying to make sense out of what she had just said to me.

"What?" I asked as I jumped up. Looking to Mignon for answers. "The night that we went to rescue Sharon, Mike. When she shot herself in the chest."

"Damn!" I said as I stood there looking down at her, sitting on the edge of my bed in tears. "Nicole, I'm so sorry to hear that. Are you okay?"

She smiled at me through her tears as she lightly nodded, letting me know that she was alright.

When she assured me she was alright, I grayly walked back over to my bedroom window, trying my best to hide my emotions, when I heard her say, "The doctor said that I should be okay after a few days or so." Her words hit a soft nerve as I wiped away a few tears that I didn't even know were there on my face.

"My goodness, I'm so sorry. And to think, you were at that damn warehouse ready to put your life back on the line for the team!" I replied as I turned to face her and Mignon, who was now seated across from us in one of my chairs, with her legs crossed, shaking her head from side to side.

Just as Mignon seen that I had wiped away a few tears, she opened her mouth with, "Michael. We still have something of importance to tell you, in regard to the team."

"And what's that, Mignon?" I asked, as if I didn't already know what was about to be said.

"We're leaving the group!"

"Yes, I already know, Mignon," I uttered as I dimly turned to face her and Nicole.

"So you knew about us leaving the group?" She asked as I stood there staring back at her and Nicole. Feeling like they had just pulled the trigger on their four nickel, hitting me directly in my stomach. With the gotdamn O'Jays, singing Stairway To Heaven, in my immediate background.

"Yes. I already knew. Your girl Strawberry told me last night. But what I need to know is, why?"

"It's nothing against you or the other girls, Michael. It's us. After this past weekend, we realize now what you were saying about the lifestyle in which we were living. In other words Michael, we don't want what we've done to come back and haunt you or any member of your prestigious group of gorgeous women that you have assembled here. Hell, we realize that in just the short time of you starting this group, you've created an Empire!"

"Indeed, haven't I?" I replied as I gave the both of them an evil smirk.

"Yes you have. And we both know that what we have started, just might cause you to lose everything."

"I see."

"And we both know that you're not having that."

"You better believe it! Not my precious Florida Hot Girls!" I said as I stared at the both of them. Then, she included as if she had forgotten.

"And oh, by the way. Entyce is leaving too."

"Yeah, she already told me. She also said that she had to do one more job before she left the group."

"What?" Mignon asked as she stood there, looking at Nicole and then me. "She said something about taking care of her snitching ass baby daddy."

"Oh shit!" Nicole uttered as she jumped up off of my bed.

"What now Nicole? I asked, looking as if something dreadful was wrong or about to happen.

"Entyce left here earlier this morning, in my car. Talking about she had something important to take care of," Nicole recited as she stood there with panic written all over her face.

"You don't think that she meant taking care of Resse, do you?"

"I have no idea, Mike. All I know is that she left here really upset about something."

"Damn! I hope that chick ain't about to do something stupid?" Mignon chimed in with as she stood to her feet. "Let's hope not. Now, who else is leaving the group?"

I asked as I could only hope and pray that Entyce hadn't left with murder on her mind.

"Just me, Nicole and Entyce. Strawberry and Tameia are staying. They both said that they were staying to continue to make them some money."

"So do you two know when it is when you're both leaving?" I asked, still shocked about all the news I was hearing at one time.

"In a few more weeks, Michael. We still want to make a few more dollars, before we head our separate ways."

"So I take it that you two aren't leaving together?"

"Nah, I'm going back to Texas, while Nicole say's that she hasn't really gave it much thought as to where she's going."

"I see."

"Once again Michael, please understand that it's not you or the group. It's just that we both feel as though we are bringing more bad than good to this group of beautiful women you have assembled around you."

"I do understand ladies and believe me, there is no hard feelings here. I truly understand what you're saying and going through," I recited as I walked over to place my arms around Mignon, then called fer Nicole.

"Hey you, please join us." We all embraced one another, until Mignon backed away with tears in the well of her seductive looking eyes. "If you ever need me to come back, you know how to get in touch with me, right?"

"Yeah, that I do Mignon."

"Same here, Michael, I'll always be just a call away," Nicole said as the both of them started walking towards the door.

Chapter 30
The Love We Had Stays On My Mind!

The both of them had just turned to the doorknob, about to step out of my room, when I yelled out to them. "Hey you two!" They both turned around at the same time, gently wiping their faces.

"Yes Michael."

"No tears you two, no tears." They both turned their lovely faces into smiles as they stood motionless for a few seconds, gazing back at me as if it was the very last time that we would all be together. Then just like that, they both walked away, with me thinking to myself about the three of them leaving the group. At first I felt like what was I going to do without them by my side, but then realized that there was always a brighter tomorrow. I closed my door, then walked back over to my bed and took a seat, listening to the Dells, singing their hit song The Love We Had Stays On My Mind. I didn't even realize that I was now singing right along with the song, reminiscing about all the good times I had with my girl Nicole.

All I knew right then that the song was saying all the things that I was now off in a daze about. Because truly and very dearly, the love I had spent with her fine ass, would always stay on my mind. So who was I fooling, things were going to be alright, I thought to myself as my cell phone began ringing, bringing me back to reality. I reached for the phone on the third ring as I seen that it was none other than my foolish ass brother, calling.

"What's up, Firstborn?"

"Nothing that a lil' money and some bad ass bitches can't handle," he said with a wicked smile on his big ass face. "And what is that supposed to mean, my wild and crazy ass brother?" I asked as I continued to sit down. "I just hit me a nice lil' lick in Tallahassee and I need to celebrate. So why don't you and Richard pack up both of your trucks and bring me all of them bad ass bitches that you call the muthafucking Florida Hot Girls!"

"Nah son, so your country ass telling me that you want to do a show, my nigga?" I voiced as a genuine smile appeared on my elated face.

"Yep and to show you how I party my nigga, we're going to do a show the entire weekend!"

I quickly jumped to my feet as I asked him. "Well damn, Friday and Saturday?"

"Yep, Chai and his brother Richard already got the spot and plenty of food locked down. So what's up? We gonna have butt naked bitches with their ass up in the air, all fucking weekend long!" He spat in sheer excitement. "So let me get this straight. You want to do a show in lil' country ass Madison, Florida?"

"You damn right, hell you have done plenty of shows here before and don't act like you too damn good for Madville. You must have forgotten that your lil' country ass was born here as well as me."

"Yeah, you're right. But you know how them jealous ass broads up there can be, once these girls I have hit that small ass town," I replied as I strolled over to my window to look outside.

"Mike, listen if I tell you to bring them badass females of yours then bring them."

It didn't even take me long to think about it, since we did need another spot to go to, since some of the ladies had did what they did in Jacksonville. Hell, it probably was the safest place for them to be that weekend. So I told him. "Alright my brother, I'm going to need at least two stacks up front in order to bring you two truckloads of beautiful, elegant, tantalizing, exotic, females. Something that small ass Madison, has never, ever seen before."

"Say no more my brother, the money will be sent by Western Union today. And oh, by the way, sexy ass Deidra told me to tell you hello. I see why you were so fucked up over her fine red ass." He recited as he grabbed at his dick, thinking of just how fine she was.

"Oh she did, huh?"

"Yes sir," he uttered, smiling from ear to ear. I could sense that there was more to what he was telling me as I cordially asked him.

"And what do you mean by that?"

"Let's just say that she really knows what to do and how to do it, in order to get what she wants, my nigga."

I turned around pissed, imagining my wild ass brother having his way with someone from my past, that I really cared about. I actually had to catch myself as I said.

"You slick mouth muthafucka! You fucked her, didn't you?"

"Damn baby brother, don't tell me that you still have some feelings for her fine red ass?" He asked me as I sat down, daydreaming about how nice it was whenever I had the pleasure of making hot, passionate love to her. "Hey, you still there?" He asked me as I snapped back with. "Nah, I just can't believe that you went there, when you know that she used to be my heart and then you go and put your dick in her."

"Man chill. If it would have been one of my old chicks, you would have done the same exact thing."

"Whatever, man. I wouldn't fuck or touch anything that you have ever fucked. Wouldn't touch them with a crackhead's dick, my nigga. Nigga just send me my bread and I'll see your ass on Friday." I had to get off of my phone, quickly, before I would have said something to really offend his black ass.

"Damn lil' bro, that's how you feel?"

"Yep."

"My bad."

"No problem."

"Well, we need the show to start around ten thirty, Friday night."

"Yeah, I hear you. Did you turn that rental in?"

"Yes and right about now, I'm in something real clean my brother. By the time you all get here this weekend, I should be sitting inside something brand new, right off the showroom floor."

"I hear you; I'll holla when we get in town"

"So, it's like that?" He asked.

"Nah, just dealing with a lot right now, that's all," I replied, lying through my teeth. He really had me in my feelings about Deidra.

"Alright, peace Mike."

"One," I said as we hung up, with me still feeling some type of way, since he had slept with one of my first loves. The conversation left me sitting there deep in thought for a few minutes, pondering over what my life might have been like if I had settled down with the girl. After a few more moments of me sitting there alone, listening to Prayin' For Time by the late great George Michael, my stomach reminded me that it was time to get something to eat. I would have gotten up at that moment, but the song had me really in my body about Deidra.

Years ago, not too many far away, I once was in love with that female that I almost went over the deep end over. You see, Deidra loved and cared about me just as much as I did her. But at that time in her complicated life, she was in love with something much more powerful than me. So powerful that it had a hold of her and wasn't going to let go. It was so powerful that I almost fell into its trap as well. I was that much in love with the girl that I was about to put myself on the line with her, just to show her how much I loved her. The bottom line was that Deidra had an addiction, a very serious addiction. And this addiction was so strong and so powerful, that it wasn't going to let her go. So at the time, I felt that I was so in love with her, that I was willing to do the same thing that she was doing. And what that was, was smoking Crack Cocaine. So there you have it, that's right. I was so in love with the girl that I was willing to smoke Crack with her, just to show her that I loved her and would do anything to be with her.

Chapter 31
Stuck In My Thoughts!

It was still early in the morning as I headed downstairs, with what I was about to cook, dancing around inside my head. Mignon and Nicole were outside by their individual cars as I looked out of the window at the both of them admiring their new whips.

"Hey, do you two want me to fix you all something to eat?" I yelled to them from the kitchen window.

"Nah, we're about to head to the mall. So we'll grab something to eat there!"

"Alright you two, be safe!" I yelled as Strawberry ran right past me, yelling. "Hey, I know y'all two chicken heads aren't about to leave without me?" While running, she turned to her right to see me standing there. "See you later, Mike." She managed to shout as she sprinted out the front door. "Hey, before I forget. Let the girls know that we have a show this weekend in Madison, Florida with my brother and some of his wild ass partners!" She abruptly stopped dead in her tracks at the mention of my brother's name.

"Oh hell nah, not with Mister Want To Fuck All Night Long!" Her eyes grew large as silver dollars as she stood there shaking.

"Yes, with his ass precisely," I replied as she lowered her head in disapproval. She then slammed the door loudly as I got the sense that her nor her swollen ass and pussy wanted to see my brother any time soon.

***

Meanwhile, over in beautiful Puerto Rico, Pierre and his brothers had received some very bad news in regards to his two eldest daughters. Nonetheless, business had to be kept in order for him and his family to remain at the top.

"So, what happened Pierre?" Felix asked his brother as he walked into his private study. Pierre was seated behind a replica of the same type of desk set-up in the hit movie, Scarface.

"I can't really say right now. All I'm sure of, is that my twenty-million-dollar jet plane went down, somewhere over the Bermuda Triangle," he said, an expensive cigar hanging out of his mouth.

"Were there any survivors, Pierre?"

"That I don't know. But what I do need to know is if my product made it safely to its destination? He said as he stood up. Seemingly as if he didn't give a flying fuck about Rhynyia, Natasha or the rest of the crew on board.

"What about the girls Pierre? Not to mention Miguel and the rest of the precious crew?" Felix asked as he stood behind his brother, confused by his actions.

"Casualties are not my main concern as of now. What mostly concerns me is the product." He spoke as he turned around. "And that my dear brother is what your mind should be on as well. You act as if your livelihood doesn't depend on the sale of what we produce," Pierre said as he put fire to the end of his cigar.

"I too am concerned Pierre, but shouldn't you at least worry about the safety of the two girls and the crew? What if the authorities or another deadly foreign factitious group had targeted them? And now has them, holding them for a nice sized ransom or something?" Pierre stared in the eyes of his brother for a moment, then gave him his signature shitty ass smirk. The one that he would give most people who got on his nerves.

"Listen my dear brother, it isn't that fucking serious. You see what has happened is that, the local authorities had got wind of my private plane being over there. Somehow instead of Rhynyia and her fucking fiancé had my plane fly into Jacksonville International, instead of Orlando. For what reasons she never got the chance to explain it to me. When they were prepared to leave Jacksonville, Florida, the authorities wanted to have the plane searched. Well that wasn't about to happen since Miguel had the plane up in the air before they got there. Now here is where the plot thickens my dear, foolish little brother," Pierre said as he was prepared to tell his brother the details. Felix sat there as if he was listening to a book being read to him. Eyes and ears opened wide as he sat.

"When Miguel found out that the plane was being followed he alerted Rhynyia, who directed him to fly over the Bermuda Triangle."

"But why was the Yayo still there on the plane with them?"

"I don't know. All I know is that they were supposed to be in Orlando, not Jacksonville," he said.

"So you think that maybe the Yayo wasn't dropped off?" Felix asked.

"Precisely. Which that if they were bringing the Yayo back, why wasn't it delivered?" Pierre stated just as one of his servants knocked on the door. "Yes come in!" He shouted. Just as he shouted, in walked a young man, who didn't look a day older than twenty-one.

"Excuse me sir?" He asked.

"Yes, what is it?"

"There is a call for you on your hotline."

"Thank you," Pierre said, then looked at Felix, "Excuse me, while I take this call.

"No problem Pierre, go ahead," Felix replied.

"Ola!" Pierre spoke into the phone, thinking that it might be some news about his precious cargo and daughters. But instead he heard the voice of …

***

Meanwhile Lil' Kitty was riding on the city bus headed to the mall, she needed to spend the money she had made from the previous weekend. And the mall was the perfect place to spend it at. She had already spent most of it, over at the Weed Man's spot. So now, with about seven hundred and sixty-five dollars to her name, she felt like splurging the rest on her and maybe one outfit for her young son. It didn't matter that her eye was still showing signs of the after effect of the fight that she had with Mo Money, either. All that mattered to her was getting over to that mall. This is where she could let off a little bit of frustration and built-up anger. But while seated on that bus, all she could think of was how Punkin had stood her up over the weekend. So without giving it a single thought, she dialed up his number. And when a female answered on the third ring, she didn't even think to just hang up.

Instead, she said, "Hello."

"Who this?" The female voice asked.

"Nah fuck who I am, who is this, answering my lil' man's phone?" She asked, chest puffed out.

"Oh, you must be calling for Punkin. Hold up!" The young woman said, then placed her hand over the receiver and spoke to someone else. "Hey, I think it's one of them lil' nasty ass tricks that Punkin was talking to before he got hit."

"Here, let me have it!" A young male said as he took the phone out of her hand. "Hello, you looking for Punkin?"

"Yeah, who is this and where is my lil' boo?"

"Right now he's talking with his Probation Officer. Is this Lil' Kitty?"

"Yeah, that's exactly who it is. And how do you know who I am, but I don't know who you are?" She asked, side smirk on her face.

"Because you all he talks about. And besides, your name is stored in his phone, right next to Wifey," the young male voiced. Just knowing the fact that Punkin had her stored in his phone, brought a wide smile to her angry face. Now she was really feeling herself.

"I see. Well how long before he's free to talk?"

"I really can't say. But I know one thing, he's really upset that he didn't get to spend some quality time with your fine ass this weekend."

"For real?" She asked, all excited and shit. "Yep, tell you what. What's your address? We are thinking about riding down to Orlando today anyway. So we gone come by and scoop you up, how about that?" Now she was really feeling herself.

"No, I tell you what. How about I jump on the next Greyhound and come up there."

"Hell, that's even better, boo. Yeah, do that. By the time you get here, we should have the room and shit. Right along with some good ass weed. Now do you have another girlfriend to come with you?"

"I sure do. I'm 'bout to call her ass right now. Matter of fact, she has her own car. So I'm just going to get her to drive up there."

"Say less. Go ahead and jump on the highway then. When y'all get here hit us back."

"No doubt," Lil' Kitty versed as she couldn't wait to see her lil' man. The only problem with that was, the damn guy was over at the local morgue, sleeping really good. Just after the guy hung up the phone, he looked over at the young lady. "See, now once her lil' dumb ass gets up here. We torture the bitch, her and her gotdamn friend. Then, we make them hoes tell us who was behind the death of my lil' brother!"

Chapter 32
Fashion!

Sharon had called me earlier to let me know that she never got the chance to take her daughter to daycare. Something about her not feeling well. So she wouldn't be back at the house that day. A situation that was perfectly okay with me, since wanting to get some alone time anyway. It was a Monday and Tuesday at Hollywood Nites lurking right around the corner. My life was already spiraling from one end to the other, with this female and that one. So I had to definitely give myself some time alone from everyone. You see I had been going back and forth to Jacksonville every weekend that we didn't have a Bachelor Party to attend and by now I had met two more females that were occupying what free time I had whenever I made it to Jacksonville.

The first female was this lil' dark skin, slim chick by the name of Felicia. Now I usually didn't date dark skinned females, but it was something about her personality that elevated me towards her. She stood around five foot six and weighed somewhere around a hundred and twenty pounds. At first, things were going okay between me and her, since I was only seeing her whenever I was in town. On a few occasions I would spend a few hours with her before I would be off to the club with my dancers. But after a few weeks she began complaining that I wasn't spending enough time with her, so she started demanding more of my time. Something that I just couldn't see myself giving to any female. The entire time that I was over in Puerto Rico, she had been blowing up my phone, wanting to know what time or when I would be returning back home. But me being so paranoid about letting individuals know where I lived, kept me from giving the girl my address. Something that I made sure I kept away from a lot of people. Good thing that I did, because she was the type of female who would just pull up on your ass in a heartbeat. While not even being invited. In short, she was about to be kicked to the muthafucking curve.

Now the second female that I was romantically tangled up with, was this beautiful fine young lady from a small ass town called, Green Cove Springs, which was located about forty five minutes outside of Jacksonville. She had the most unusual name that I had ever heard, along with one of the most gorgeous smiles that a single man would welcome to witness. Her name was Fashion and that's exactly what she looked like, a beautiful runway Fashion Model. This elegant looking vixen stood five foot eight, with a nice athletic toned body, banging body as if she was a World Class Sprinter. And she weighed an amazing hundred and thirty-five pounds, with a beautiful pecan tan complexion to boot.

Whenever I was dodging Felicia or any of the other ladies in the group who I might be with that particular weekend, I was deliriously involved with my girl, Fashion. Now she could have popped up at my house any time she wanted, and I wouldn't have given a damn. Since I was home by myself, I had actually forgotten how nice it felt to be alone. Now that Sharon wasn't coming back over, I thought about calling Fashion and inviting her down to my place for dinner. But then I thought twice about that idea and simply fell asleep right after I had fixed myself something to eat.

A few hours later, I was awoken by my phone ringing off of the hook. At first I wasn't going to answer it, but after it stopped ringing, it started once again. 'Damn, whoever this is must really need to speak with me.' I thought to myself. Then realizing that I hadn't heard from Rhynyia as of yet, so what if it was her.

"Hello." I quickly answered.

"Michael."

"Yeah, who is this?" I asked as I laid there, mind wondering.

"It's me, Felicia."

My lips curled up and my attitude dropped.

"Oh, what's good?" I asked, now really wanting to go back to sleep. But what she said next, was about to throw my entire mental off. "Were you busy?"

"Nah, just getting some rest, that's all."

"I see. So, why didn't you come by this weekend, since you and them hoes were up here in town?" She asked.

"What are you talking about? And how do you know we were in town?"

"Don't worry about how I know. Just know that I know every move you make, whenever you're in my city."

"I see. Don't let me find out that you have somebody watching me?" I stated as I rolled out of bed.

"Don't worry, if I did you will never know," she versed.

I would find out later that she did have someone watching out for me. It was her gotdamn aunt, who worked at the damn hotel we always stayed at.

"Anyway Michael, I have something to tell you."

"What now, Felicia? And no, I don't have any money to spare," I said as I took a deep breath, then let it out.

"I'm pregnant with your child. That's what, my nigga!"

"Damn! Damn! Damn!" Not this chick, I said to myself as I was really about to hate my life, because Felicia was not some female who I wanted to have a kid with.

No sir, not this chick. It could have been any other chick I was sleeping with, but not Felicia. Felicia was not the one, hell, I didn't even want anyone to see me with the chick. I don't even know why in the hell I was fucking with her trifling ass. All she saw in her eyes now was a paycheck. Or should I say, Child Support check.

"Hello, are you still there?" She asked me as I could see the smile on her face through my phone. And at that time there was no such thing as FaceTime.

"Yeah, I'm still here, Felicia. How certain are you that it's my baby?" I asked, praying that she could see the sad look on my face.

"Believe me, it's yours," she said. "You're the only person that I have been with, Michael." She continued with.

"Yeah, right," I replied, sounding all disgusted and shit.

"You are. Now what I want to know is are you going to be there for your child, Michael? "

"Yeah Felicia, I have to go. Bye Felicia," I said, then just hung up on her ass. Now what in the hell was I going to do now? This is when I took another deep breath, then let it out, feeling like straight shit. Now if my girl Fashion was having my child, that wouldn't be a problem. Because Fashion was all that and a bag of chips. To be honest with you, she ranked right at the top of my list, right along with Rhynyia, Sharon and Nicole. Hell, I even wanted to take her by my parents' house and introduce her to my mother and father. The only problem with that was the simple fact of me not really having the time to do it. It didn't matter anyway; my mother wouldn't have wanted to meet her at all. That's just the way she was, when it came to me. I guess she always felt like there wasn't a woman out there that I was dealing with that was good enough to be with her son. Truth be told, she just felt like I was dealing with too many women and didn't want to meet any of them. Bless her heart she would always ask to tell me.

"Mike, I don't know where you got your whorish ways from."

My answer would always be the same. "Me neither, mother. Me neither."

Chapter 33
Sharing Locations!

Now remember how I said during the book, how I didn't like for my ladies to give out their number? But one in particular always did. Well, this is how she stopped. Because what I'm about to tell you caused her lil' thin ass to always have second thoughts after this ordeal. Now, just as her ass had got off of the phone with the dude in Jacksonville, she called her ride or die best friend. The female picked up on the first ring.

"What it do, Lil' Kitty?" She asked "Hey, remember the lil' dude I was telling you about in Jacksonville?"

"Which one Lil' Kitty, you meet so many?" Her friend asked.

"My boo, the dude they call Punkin," she said.

"Oh, yeah I remember, what about him?"

"Well get this. I just talked to one of his partners and they want us to come up there and chill, smoke some Trees and just ball out! They even claim they have some bread to throw at our feet," she lied, trying her best to entice her friend to say okay, which was all because the chick had a car,

"Okay, when we rolling up there? And what about Mike? You know he hasn't called my ass since the night he fired me over at the Caribbean Nightclub?" Ms. Ceily asked

"It doesn't matter. Fuck Mike and his lil' bitch Mo Money. I'm about to tell him and the Hot Girls that they can kiss my ass. Fuck it, I can do this shit on my own!" She barked. Not knowing what she was about to get them into.

"Oh shit, what happened now, Lil' Kitty? Because ever since I have known your lil' short ass, when shit don't go your way, you become pissed off, like you sound right about now."

"Fuck all that! Do you want to go make this money or what? You know that you can stay your broke, black ass here and not make shit."

"Who said that I don't want to go? How we getting up there? You know my bucket of a car might not make it all the way up to Duval?"

"Girl stop! Your car will make it up there. Don't worry about the gas or outfit. I have all of that. Now just come scoop me up over at the Florida Mall. I just got here, so I'm 'bout to grab you an outfit to dance in. You cool with that?"

A wide smile emerged on Ceily's face as she came back with. "Hell yeah, hey can I bring along a few more girls too?"

"Hell yeah, the more, the better. Shittttt, the way I see it is. We can just stay up there for the entire week and make nothing but bread."

***

Just as Trigger hung the phone he looked over at the female who answered Punkin's phone. "I think we got one. Let me make this quick call to make sure though," he uttered as he dialed the number. Tracey answered on the very first ring.

"Hello Trigger, what's up?"

"Hey, have you ever heard the name Lil' Kitty?"

She paused for a moment, running the name through her memory bank. "Not really, but I have seen that number in your brother's cell phone," she replied, mental still spinning. For some reason, she knew that she had heard that particular name, recently. Had even heard it within the last few days, but where? She knew if she could remember where she heard the name before, she just might be able to put a face with the name, "Well, get this. I just got off of the phone with her ass. I was able to talk her and a couple of her girlfriends to drive up here to Duval."

"Okay, so what does that have to do with me?" She asked, still heartbroken over her loss.

"It's like this, once she gets here, me and the crew gone put our thang down. I was thinking that maybe we have you see her face and then, we might be able to find out what happened to Punkin and why?"

"Yeah Trigger, that sounds good and shit! But I know what got his lil' ass murked! Him and his lil' ass dick. Always out here in these streets tricking with the lil' dope money he be making, when his dead ass should have been here with me and his lil' son!" She said as her tears began to attack her eyes. The poor girl was still hurting. Hurting was really an understatement. Tracey was crushed.

"Listen, Tracey, I do hear you and no one is hurting more than me. Hell, that was my gotdamn brother! Now, he's gone. And the way I see it, this shit ain't over, until me and my crew find the culprits behind it. Now either you down with what we are about to do or not? It's your choice," he said as he had tears of his own, strolling down his face.

"Do what you have to do, Trigger. Just call me when the bitch gets here. Let me get off this phone. You do know that now I have to plan on how we are going to bury his ass," she said as she cried.

"Hold on, you know the one dude he rolled with? The guy who owned the Rib Joint."

"Yeah, I know him. But didn't they get his ass over at the hospital?"

"Yes, they did. But his family says that they're paying for everyone's funeral."

"Is that so?" She asked, with a bit of hope at the end of the tunnel. "Yes, I'm about to shoot you the number. From there you all can discuss the burial arrangements."

"Alright Trigger, and thanks."

"No problem, sis. Have your phone on, when that bitch gets here, I'm gone snap a pic and send it to you. Then maybe, something might click."

"Okay," she spoke softly, as the both of them hung up. Just as she did, lil' Junior walked into her arms, looking just like his father. Now Tracey was really feeling the loss of the young man she was supposed to get married to, sometime in the near future. All of that was now just a memory as she sat there, holding on tight to all she had left of Punkin. Her mind and mental were all a drift as she reminisced about Punkin.

"Mommy, when is my daddy coming back home?" The little man asked, snapping her back to reality. The little man was still just a tot and Tracey really didn't know how to tell the young man that his father wasn't coming back. "Mommy, do you hear me?" He asked as he turned to look up into her face. Just as she witnessed his small eyes, she broke back down. Looking into her son's eyes caused the woman nothing but pain, for Punkin and his young son looked exactly alike. People would always say that Tracey must have been angry at the man while she carried his son, since he resembled his father so much.

* * *

Meanwhile, down at the Police Station, the place was like a madhouse. The city was preparing for their first Super Bowl, but all of that was about to be threatened by the growing numbers of senseless murders throughout the ever-growing city.

The Police Chief was holding his daily Press Conference, and he knew that the reporters were going to be asking him about the growing number of senseless killings. He thought that he was prepared, and he was, up until one of the reporters asked him.

"Excuse me Chief, Brad Stevens with the Daily Journal! Do you think that all of these killings in some way might be connected with each other? First there was the murder of two men over at the hotel off of Interstate 10, then there was the murder over at that rundown warehouse. Now we have another just over the weekend at the hospital." The Chief was now overcome with anxiety as he stood at the podium. Eyes roaming the crowd as if he was looking for someone to help him answer the barrage of questions coming his way.

"I can't say right now. But I do know this. My detectives are working around the clock in regard to all of these killings," he spoke, voice cracking as he stood there.

"Are there any leads in these killings?" Another reporter asked. She was a young-looking white female. The Chief had never seen her before.

"Only a few. And the ones we do have you all already know of," he replied.

"Is it true that the perpetrators might be women?" That same attractive reporter asked.

"There are some that think that, but we can only speculate since we are still going over the footage from the hospital."

"What about the killings that are taking place after some of the strippers are leaving the club that they work at?" Another reporter asked.

"Excuse me?" He asked, not even knowing about those killings.

"The Strippers. Seems as though there has been about three women who have been found mutilated and raped before being killed."

"To my knowledge, my department hasn't been informed of anything such as this," he spoke, now really confused.

"So Chief, you're not aware of all of these particular murders?"

"No. Not a one. And this Press Conference is over! If you want these cases to be solved, please let me get back to work!" He stated as he stormed off the podium.

Just as he stepped down, he was greeted by the City Mayor. He had a cigar in his mouth and sheer concern written all over his face.

"Mayor! I didn't know you were here! The Chief blurted out.

"I know, that's the way I needed it to be. There was no way in hell that I could have stood up there and took all of those questions," the Mayor said. Then continued with. "So, you mean to tell me that you nor your department know about the Taxicab murders?"

"The what?" The Chief asked. He had never heard of anything remotely about what he had just been asked.

"They are calling them the Taxicab killings. And I guess the reason you haven't heard about them is because they have been happening on the other side of the bridge," the Mayor stated as they both walked into the Chief's office.

Chapter 34

To Entyce A Rat!

Reese was really feeling himself right about now, since the first woman that he had ever loved, had called him. Even though the detectives had warned him to not tell anyone where he laid his head now, he did. She had told him that she really needed to speak to him. So, he fell for the lie. At first, he actually did think twice about it. Asking himself, what if it was set-up or something? What if it was all a plot to have him come out of hiding? But when she told him that it was about the baby and how they needed to get a place of their own, he had a change of heart and fell for the bold-faced lie.

He had agreed to meet up with her, not even realizing that she knew about him being a life-sized human rat. The address that he had given Entyce had her puzzled as she asked herself. 'Now who in the hell does he stay with out here in these nice ass homes? And who in their right mind would let his broke ass live with them?' She mumbled all of this as she pulled up into the driveway, then turned off the engine to Nicole's car. Just as she had cheeked her weapon of choice, she dialed his number. He answered on the first ring, with.

"What it do?"

"I'm outside," she softly spoke. Her heart was laced with murder. "Alright, come on up to the door, I'll open it for you." He spoke back into the phone. Entyce then made sure the silencer fitted nice and tugged on her weapon. Just as she did, she stepped out of the car, dressed in all black, head to toe.

"Okay Entyce, you can do this!" She uttered out loud as she turned the corner of the driveway. A few steps away she was at the door of the lovely home, nestled inside of a well kept Cul-de-sec at the end of the street.

Her plan to kill her baby's father was flawless, she wasn't going to tarry with the man for long at all. Just when he opened the door and turned away to walk inside of the house, she was going to blow his brains out and leave the man stanking right there in the middle of the foyer. All of this might have taken place, and she would have rid me and the group of the man snitching on us. But just as she got to the front door, she happened to see a door camera pointed directly into her face. So that plan was quickly banished from her train of thought. Now, what was she to do?

"Damn!" She voiced, just as he came to the door, face holding a giant smile.

"Hello beautiful?" He greeted her by saying.

She took a deep breath, then sighed. "Hello, Reese. How are you?" She asked, heart now racing. She only wanted to be here for about ten minutes. But by the smile he had placed on his face, she now knew that her time here would be a while.

"Come on in," he said.

"Thank you," she replied as she stepped inside the home. It smelt like weed.

"Welcome to my humble abode."

Now looking around she knew that this place couldn't be his.

"So, who do you stay here with?" She asked as she now stood inside the living room.

"Who do you think?" He asked as he walked over to where it looked like he was sitting before she arrived. "Have a seat." He told her as he sat down and picked up the rest of the blunt he was smoking.

"Because the last time I checked, your ass didn't have a job. So I know this place isn't yours," she voiced as she knew gotdamn well who the place belonged to. Now what we all knew was true, was apparent to her. Her baby daddy was an official rat and was now living the high life.

"No, it isn't mine. You already know what it is, Entyce," he said, not trying to lie to her at all. But what he said next, gave her the green light, on sparing his life. "And before you pull that pistol out and blow my brains out, you nor the people you work with have to worry. I'm not squealing at all! Why would I? Mike has been nothing but good to me ever since me meeting you guys. So let him know that I'm only using these people since I don't have nowhere else to go."

"So you think that I'm here to kill you?" She asked as she batted her fake eyelashes.

"Yes, my dear. Now let's go outside to the pool area. I don't need them people to hear what I have to tell you."

"But you have already said a mouthful," she voiced. "That's why the television is turned up. They couldn't hear what I was saying, that's why I had my hand up to my mouth. That was in case they were trying to read my lips." Just as he said that, he stood up and took her hand, now leading her out to the pool area.

***

Back over at the police station, the Mayor had just told the Chief about the other killings. And the only reason why he wasn't angry with the Chief was all because how would he know about them, if he was too busy trying to solve his own murder cases?

"So many people believe that these killings have been done by women," the Mayor spoke. "Well the footage from the hospital does confirm that. But we just can't see who the women might be, since every one of them had their faces covered," the Major said.

"I know. I asked my two officers why they didn't ask to see their faces and they both said that they were occupied by something else," the Chief stated.

"I know maybe they were both too busy trying to see what their bodies looked like. I saw the footage as well. And I must admit, their bodies were banging!" The Mayor said, eyes trained in on the Chief.

"That they were. And that is the same reason why those two officers are both unemployed at this very moment. A young man is dead and gone all because those two couldn't control their sexual intentions. The black officer Murray actually had a gotdamn orgasm right there in front of both of the fake officers who clearly looked like strippers in those fake officer outfits," Chief said not realizing that he had just uttered the key to the puzzle right there, as he spoke with the Mayor.

"Let me ask you something though, Cliff."

Cliff was the name of the Chief.

"What's that Ralph?"

"You know, just a few days ago, down in Daytona, there was a killing, almost execution style, that took place at Red Lobster," Ralph said.

"Okay, what does that have to do with the killings up here in Duval?" Cliff asked.

"The guy that got killed was from here. A highly decorated ex-Military guy."

"Okay."

"Well get this, he was gunned down by a group of women. What if those women were the same women that just left that poor black man dead?" The Mayor asked as he sat there, staring at the Chief, both men frozen stiff as they tried to put a case together. Quickly reaching for his desk phone, Cliff picked it up. "What are you doing?"

"I need to see the footage from the shooting in Daytona."

"But what about the footage here? You think that it might add up?" The Mayor asked with his skepticism on high alert.

"I don't know, but if there is any way that the females that did the killings in Daytona match up with the ones here, we might have our first break into these senseless killings," Cliff recited as he waited for someone to answer on the other line of his phone.

"Media room, Officer Bart Ferguson speaking," the voice said.

"Hey Bart, this is the Chief. Do you have the footage of a shooting that happened down in Daytona, Beach? At a Red Lobster?"

"Let me check the system, give me a few moments, Chief," the man uttered as the Chief placed his hand over the receiver and spoke to the Mayor.

"He's checking for the footage right now!"

"Good, I want this case closed ASAP!" The Mayor told him as he sipped on his third cup of coffee.

"Okay, looks like I do have some of the footage of that crime. Is there anything else that I can help you with, Chief?" Bart asked as he sat at his desk, staring at the monitor.

"Yes. The footage of the heinous murder that took place over at the hospital," Chief asked, now feeling like he himself, was about to crack a case. Something he hadn't did since becoming the Chief of Police ten long years ago. Chief even had a wicked smirk on his face as he sat there. Now reaching for his cup of coffee as well.

"Sorry Chief, I don't have any footage on file or even seen the actual footage."

"What in the hell happened to it?" He shouted as spittle flew out of his mouth.

"I have no idea, but it looks like it was signed out by an officer by the name of …" Bart mumbled the name. He was mumbling so fucking low, that the Chief had to ask him.

"Who, speak up son?" Chief was irate at the moment. "It was signed out by Officer. Get this Chief," Bart said, then continued with. "Officer Alexander Nevermind."

Chapter 35
Guardian Angels!

Nicole and Mignon were just pulling into the parking lot of the Florida Mall. The same exact mall where Lil' Kitty was walking her lil' hot ass out of with both hands filled with shopping bags. Her small face lit up just as she witnessed Ms. Ceily whipping the corner in her beat-up ass car. I think her car was a white Falcon, 1978 model at that.

"Hey chick, isn't that hot ass Lil' Kitty right there?" Nicole asked as she pointed at Lil' Kitty with her right index finger.

"Where?" Mignon asked, breaking her attention span on trying to get a parking spot.

"Right there and by the looks of it, she's getting inside that white beat up ass car. What kind of car is that?" Nicole asked, with a surprised look on her face.

"Oh, I see her. Hell, don't ask me to lie. I don't know what kind of raggedy ass car that is. But isn't that the chick that Mike fired that night over at the Caribbean Beach Nightclub?"

Nicole looked hard and long, then uttered. "Damn sho is Ms. Ceily. I wonder what they're up to." Nicole asked as she looked over at her partner in crime.

"I don't know, but whatever it is, it looks like they're up to no good. Especially if Lil' Kitty is in the mix," Mignon versed.

"So what, do we follow them or what? Nicole asked as she eased back inside the plush leather seat of the Benz.

"Why shitttt! I'm here to buy me a couple of outfits for the weekend," Mignon stated.

"Me too, for all that matters. But for some reason, I think those chicks are about to get in some serious ass trouble," Nicole said as she began counting the number inside the white bucket.

"Trouble like what, Nicole? And besides, whatever trouble they are about to get in has nothing to do with us. Let's just go shopping like we planned," Mignon versed.

"Hold up, she might have a point there, Mignon. Maybe we should follow them. Who knows, we might just be their Guardian Angels," Strawberry said from the back seat.

"I think she's right, Mignon. And by some of the faces of the chicks in that car. It looks like some of them chicks that Mike used to have with us," Nicole said.

"Which ones?"

"It looks like them Bout It Bout It chicks," Nicole said to Mignon.

"Well whoever it is, if you don't hurry up and get behind them, we might know where they're going," Strawberry said as she sat up in the back seat. "Okay, but look around us, if them dumb ass broads about to get into some trouble, we are a couple of girls short," Mignon stated as she put her Benz in reverse, then got about four car lengths behind the white Falcon.

"Oh well. Whatever we have to get into we just make sure we can handle it. Now is our gear in the trunk?" Nicole asked, eager to find out what Lil' Kitty and her friends had going on.

"Yep! Everything we might need is in the trunk," Mignon told her as they mentally prepared for whatever might lay ahead for them.

Up ahead, inside the white Falcon, Lil' Kitty was so hyped up with anticipation of seeing her lil' boo, she didn't even realize that she was now riding in the car with some real grimy ass bitches. All whom were from that group I had to let go earlier. The Bout It Bout It Girls. Now these chicks were down with doing just about anything for whatever amount of money they were to receive. And Lil' Kitty might have wanted to re-think her plan of just allowing any group of girls traveling with her and Ms. Ceily. But at the moment, all she cared about was getting her lil' hot ass back to Duvall. She just had to see Punkin. "So how we looking on gas, girl?" Lil' Kitty asked Ms. Ceily.

"I only had two dollars while the chicks in the backseat didn't have any money at all."

"Ahhh, hell nah! So you hoes ain't got no money for gas, but y'all want to ride with us?" Lil' Kitty barked as she turned her head, to see four thirsty ass females, dressed in barely anything. First, there was this one lil' slim, dark-skinned chick, who went by the name of Eat'em Up! You can already guess why they called her that. Then, sitting next to her was her baby sister. She was a light skinned pretty female, who was probably the finest one in the car. Her name was Ass Eater. Yeah, you already know. She was damn good at it too. But for some reason she couldn't figure out why her breath was always stinking.

Seated right next to Ass Eater was this other chick that the projects loved. That's why they gave her the nickname Project Hoe. And last but not least, was this one lil' hottie named Keisha. Keisha was just eighteen years of age and had already had five kids to raise and take care of so you know she would do just about anything for a small piece of change.

"Damn Lil' Kitty, why we got to be all of that? We just trying to make a lil' money too. But I promise you just as soon as we make this bread that we are about to make we will all pay you back," Keisha spoke for the entire group as she sat there with her pussy ready to be fucked.

"No problem, just as long as you hoes pay my ass back? Now you, I got you two outfits. I hope you like them?" Lil' Kitty said to Ms. Ceily.

"That's cool girl. But before I check them out we need to pull over and get some gas," she said as she pulled over to the gas station on Orange Blossom Trail.

"No problem, here. Fill up the tank. Do you girls need something out of the store?" Lil' Kitty asked. Her thin ass leg hanging out of the whip.

"Yeah, hold up! Since you paying, let me come inside with you," Keisha muttered as she jumped out, now following right behind Ms. Ceily and Lil' Kitty. Before it was said and done everyone had got out of the car all except Ass Eater.

"Hey Keisha, tell my sister to pick me up some gum!"

"Yeah, will do!" Keisha shouted back, then mumbling under her breath with. 'I'm glad you realized that your ass needs some gum, hoe!"

Now with all of them inside the store, Mignon slowly pulled up to the gas pump. Then rolled her window down and shouted. "Hey where the party at?"

"I don't know but me and my girls are headed up to Jacksonville. My girl Lil' Kitty claims that her nigga, Punkin and his crew wants to spend some money with us!"

"Well damn! Well. I guess you all have enough heads, huh?"

"Yes we do! You know only so much money can be spent!" Ass Eater shouted as Mignon looked over at Nicole then Strawberry. "Well I guess we know what them hoes are about to get into!"

"'For sho!" Nicole replied as she shook her head from side to side in disgust. "This bitch just will not leave well enough alone."

"I know that's right. So whoever has Punkin's phone must have seen that he had been talking with her trifling ass. Now her and them poor girls are walking straight into a trap of some sort," Nicole said.

"Not only that once they have them up there they just might torture them all right before they kill them," Strawberry uttered from the back seat.

And that's exactly what those guys had in mind. If only Lil' Kitty had just left well enough alone. Don't get me wrong though, some of the girls in the group felt like she should get what she wanted, since she was always into something. Remember we lost one of the most profitable spots because of Lil' Kitty and Ms. Ceily. Then, there were all the arguments and fighting amongst the group. In the end, Lil' Kitty was always right there in the middle of every terrible situation. But still, there was no way that I wanted her to be put out of the group like this. No way, not here. Even though she had did a lot and had a big mouth, she was still one of my number one girls and there was no way that I wanted any harm brought to her on my watch. But just maybe, what if Lil' Kitty and her friends had a date with death? And who was I to stop them from making their appointment? Damn, Lil' Kitty, damn, damn, damn!

Chapter 36
Re-up!

Right after my foolish ass brother hung up the phone with me, he made a call over to Puerto Rico. It seemed as though he was moving the weight faster than he thought. So fucking fast that he decided to call Pierre and tell him that he needed to come back over to Puerto Rico so that he could re-up.

"So you say that you're moving the product like that my friend?" Pierre asked him as he placed his hand over the receiver and whispered to his brother, Felix with. "The product was delivered. This is Firstborn on the phone."

"Good," Felix replied.

"Hell yeah! This shit selling like Hotcakes on a Saturday morning!" Firstborn said back into the phone.

"That's good to hear my friend. So, how much of it have you moved?" Pierre asked as he stood up, then gazed out of his office window, looking down at the many people he had working for him.

"Enough. That's why I need to come back over, so that I can re-up. Is that cool with you?" Firstborn asked.

"Certainly, why would it be a problem? You seen for yourself how much product we have."

"I sure did," Firstborn uttered.

"Well then, what day should I expect you back over here and are you bringing your brother with you as well?"

"In a few days, maybe on Wednesday. And as far as he is concerned, I don't think that my little brother wants to get his hands dirty. You get my drift?" Firstborn stated.

"I see. And Wednesday should be fine," Pierre said with a side smirk on his face.

"Cool then, I guess I'll see you in a few days. And by the way, did the girls make it back safe and sound?" He asked as Pierre paused for a brief minute. Then said, "I don't know how to tell you this young man. But let me try. It seems as though when they left Florida, they had to avert their flight plan, somehow the authorities got wind of my plane being there."

"So, what are you saying, sir? They didn't make it back?" Firstborn asked as his heart dropped. Miguel had to fly the plane over the Bermuda Triangle. And we haven't heard from them as of yet." was all he said as Firstborn fell hard to the bed. "I have to call my brother; I'll talk with you soon." was all he said as he hung up.

***

It had been a few hours since I had talked to my brother and when I saw that he was calling me again, he was the last person that I wanted to speak to. So I just hit the end button and sent his ass straight to voicemail. But just as soon as I hit the end button, he called right back. I still didn't answer, with me being in my feelings and all, why should I? I said to myself as I turned off the volume of my phone.

"Fuck him!" I said out loud as I rolled over in bed, now searching for my remote to the television, not even pondering what it was that his ass wanted.

So I laid there in bed, still with that uneasy feeling as if something was wrong or about to happen. Deep down I knew that I wasn't feeling this way for nothing. It had to be something very serious for me to feel this way. Ever since my conscience revealed himself, the feeling came naturally. But as I lay there now, there was nothing. Just me and my mental off to ourselves, lost, wondering and waiting for sheer disaster. Who would have ever thought that one of my precious females was secretly behind my back about to bring my Empire to the fucking ground? It was mad crazy that the entire time that she had been in the group, I never knew that she felt the way she did. All in all, I never seen the writing on the wall. I guess it had been there, ever since that day when Rhynyia and I had to send her lil' cute ass back home.

Now don't get it twisted, it wasn't Phyllis, Innocence who had the knife in my back, it was someone else who I least expected it to be. And I knew it, I just didn't know that it would be her who did it. Or maybe I just thought that she was cut from a much different cloth than the rest of us was. Like they always say, that's what I got for thinking. I wouldn't find out until later when it all went down as to what she had put in play. The vicious cutthroat move she orchestrated was that she called the local Police Department in Jacksonville, Florida and told them that me and Malik were running an elite prostitution ring in their city and that whenever I would arrive back in Duval, me and the girls would be staying over at the Laquinta Inn, right off of Baymeadows.

And since the Chief and Mayor were trying their best to clean up the city, the Chief himself had the Sheriff put together an undercover operation. They gave the shit a name, but who cared? I was the main object of the entire investigation, with Malik being the guy who supplied the guys. I guess you can say that the chick in my group really had it out for me and played it off all so well. Sad thing about all of that was the simple fact that all of that bullshit was a gotdamn lie. And if I would have known that this certain female was behind my back setting me up, I would have let her ass go a long time ago. All up in my face pretending to be that one female in the group who wanted to be a manager and shit. I guess some things are not as evident as other things are. Or maybe I should have just paid close attention to those who I kept around me. Then I could have seen the enemy right in front of me. Instead, she played her snake ass role to the T.

***

Meanwhile, back up in Duval, Lil' Breezy and his big cousin Breezy had been mourning the loss of their big homie. They had known the man ever since they all were small kids playing in the sandbox, shooting marbles and chasing little girls ponytails. They had grown so close to one another that they simply called themselves brothers. Even though they weren't brothers at all.

Whenever Lil' Breezy and his cousin didn't have anything to eat they would run over to Marquise's place and eat. His mother adored the boys and always told them that their house was their house. Years later when things got bad for Lil' Breezy and Big Breezy, they moved back to North Carolina with their grandmother. She tried to raise the boys as best as she could, but you know how young boys who think they're men can be. When they reached the age of eighteen, they would travel back and forth from North Carolina to Jacksonville, Florida. Now with Marquise gone, the only thing they felt that they could do to get over the pain and loss was to track down whomever it was behind the hideous, gruesome murder.

"You know if you would have been in place the other night we too might be dead with the big homie and his crew," Lil' Breezy told his cousin as he drove down the interstate.

"Yeah, I'm glad that my black ass wasn't in place. If so, granny might be looking for a casket for our asses too," Big Breezy replied as he smoked on some purple Kush weed. "You want to hit this lil' cuz?" he asked his cousin, his eyes half closed.

"Nah man, I'm driving and I need my mind clear when I pull up on this bitch," Lil' Breezy said.

"That's what I wanted to ask you before I got in this car. Where in the hell are we going?" He asked his cousin.

"Nigga just sit back and chill. You want to get to the bottom of this shit, don't you?"

"Yeah, but where are we headed nigga? We've been on the road for at least two hours?" Big Breezy asked as they passed the Santora exit, on Interstate 4.

"The other day, when we were at the hospital, and those fake ass cops came and snatched up ole girl," Lil' Breezy said.

"Yeah, so what?"

"Well when the lil' bitch got up to use the bathroom I went inside the bitches purse."

"Okay, did you get any money?"

"Nah, but I got her address," Lil' Breezy replied.

"So, that's where we're headed?"

"Gotdamn right, we gone pull up on this bitch and make her ass show us where the rest of her crew is located," Lil' Breezy spat with venom, coming out of his mouth.

"But nigga, are we strapped like that? I don't have my piece on me right now," Big Breezy asked as he eased up inside the passenger seat.

"Everything is in the trunk, my boy. Now sit back and let me handle this," Lil' Breezy said as he flew past the first Orlando exit. He had drove the entire time, not letting Big Breezy know that they were about to commit mass murder. Just a few miles up the Interstate, Lil' Breezy saw the exit he needed to get off on. The sign read OBT exit, which stood for Orange Blossom Trail. It was one of the most dangerous places to be in Orlando.

"Okay, now we're getting somewhere," Lil' Breezy said as he pulled off of the exit. Once off of the exit, he pulled up into what looked like a Project. "Hold tight cousin, watch this," he told Big Breezy.

"Alright nigga, don't get us down here to get fucked up!"

"That's just what I don't want. Now hold up, let me holla at these dudes right here for a minute," he said as he rolled down the window and shouted out to a few fellas that were seated around a big ass Oak Tree.

"Hey mane, do you guys know where I can find a female by the name of Breshia Thomas?"

There were about four guys around the tree. None of them knew a Breshia Thomas aka Mo Money. That was because I gave her the nickname Mo Money. A few of the guys in the neighborhood knew her by Mo Money, but the two would-be killers didn't know that. All Lil' Breezy knew was Breshia.

The guys around the tree looked from one another neither one of them knowing a damn thing about the person they were asking for. Freddie B was from Mercy Drive. He was fresh out of the Pen and needed some quick paper. His pockets were light. This is when he looked over to the guys and said amongst them. "These niggas look like they ain't from around here. So, follow my lead."

"What you 'bout to do, Freddie B?" Lester Jackson asked. He was down for anything and if Freddie B said follow his lead, he would.

"Yo, where you guys from?" Freddie B asked as he walked up to the car.

Lil Breezy saw the hands of his cousin twitch. "Yo Breezy, stay cool man. I got this."

Just as Freddie B got to the passenger window, Lil' Breezy hit the man with a side smirk. "We from Duval, bruh. Just came down to chill with Breshia and a few other homegirls."

"Oh, okay. Tell you what, follow me and the homies up the road. I'll show you where she lives."

"Cool," Lil' Breezy spoke as Freddie B turned around yelling over to Poppa.

"Yo Poppa, throw me your keys!" Poppa had just bought an old school Cutlass and there was no way that he was about to give his car to Freddie B. Hell, Freddie B didn't even have a gotdamn license.

"Nigga fuck that! Tell you what. Whatever you 'bout to do to these fools, we all in," Poppa spoke as he looked from one greasy face to the other. "You niggas cool with that?"

"Hell yeah!" Curtis Williams shouted.

He was always down with whatever. And if it meant jacking another nigga, he was down with whatever. He was the one nigga who always wanted to rob a nigga. Not realizing that this just might be the wrong nigga to fuck with it.

Chapter 37
The Ying-Yang Twins!

I waited for about two hours before I turned my cell phone volume back up. I'm glad that I did because just as soon as I turned it up, Mignon was calling me.

"Yeah, what's up?" I asked her as I turned the volume on the television. "Yo, Mike."

"Yeah Mignon," I replied, due to the way she sounded. Whenever she sounded like that, there was trouble coming behind it. "I think your girl and a few of her partners are about to travel up to Duval."

"Why you say that?"

"We we're over at the Florida Mall and seen her ass get in the car with Ms. Ceily and shit."

"Okay."

"Well we followed them to a gas station. When they all went inside, we asked the one girl who was still in the car. I think it was that one chick that they call Ass Eater."

"Talking about the one lil' cute red one, right?"

"Yeah, her Mike. Now, will you please listen?"

"Yeah, go head," I replied as I eased up in bed.

"Well she's the one who told us that they're on their way up to Jacksonville, something about Lil' Kitty having some nigga that wants to see her," Mignon said.

"That can't be good. But hold on, my phone just beeped." I told her as I quickly clicked over. "Hello."

"Hey Mike, what's good playa?" The familiar voice asked over the phone.

"Nothing much kid, what cha got going on?" I asked. I knew it had to be important since this cat only called me whenever he needed me and the girls in his city.

"I'm doing a big show up here Wednesday night with this up-and-coming rap group and we need your girls up here in the place to be," he said, sounding all excited and shit.

"Wednesday night, huh?" I said as I began to formulate the amount of money I was about to ask for inside my head. Already knowing that I would agree to bring the girls, since we didn't have the Caribbean Beach Nightclub anymore. "Yeah can you and those bad ass ladies make it?"

"What's the ticket?" I asked. He then said the magic words.

"Whatever your price is, Mike. You know I got it," he replied as I could see the young brother smiling through my phone. And we didn't even have FaceTime at that present time.

"You know the deal. Send me the hundred up front so that I can lock your day in, and I'll pick up the remaining seven hundred when we get there," I told him as I sat there rubbing my hands together. Always ready to collect some paper.

"Say less Mike, you know what club it is, right?"

"Yeah, the Venue, right?"

"Yes sir."

"Cool, I'll see you then." I told him and then clicked back over to Mignon. I had to find out what was really going on. "Mignon."

"Yeah, Mike. I hope that that call was really important," she said, sounding all disgusted and shit.

"Nah girl, that was your boy up in Gainesville. He needs you and the rest of the girls in in town on Wednesday night, he says that there's some up-and-coming rap group that's going to be in town at their club."

"So what, we're going right?"

"Yeah Mignon, we're going. Now stop Lil' Kitty and them dumb ass females from going to Jacksonville. Because we don't know what may happen to them when they get there."

"You're right and we most definitely don't need her finding out about what took place over the weekend. Not like this. Because her lil' ass might put two and two together and then we might have to kill her for not keeping her fucking mouth closed."

"You're right, Mike. We got this. See you back at the house later on."

"Okay Mignon, be safe," I told her as we hung up. Just as I did I took a deep breath and then exhaled. Shit was really becoming hectic for me and the girls and what was more bizarre than that was the fact that I still hadn't heard from my precious Rhynyia yet. Here it was that I didn't know if she was safe and sound or had even made it home yet. So to ease my mind and fear, I decided to give her a quick call.

***

The four guys were so eager to rob someone that neither one of them even thought about who these guys were and how they got down. Nah, not today. Today was the day that these guys had murder and mayhem on their minds.

"So, where we taking these niggas at, Poppa?" Curtis asked from the back seat. He was in the back seat loading up his forty-five. He was the brother who never left the house without his piece.

"It's a spot outside of Orlando, right down the road from Apopka. Once we get these Bama ass niggas out there, we gone smoke their black asses! Y'all down with that?" Poppa asked as he drove through traffic.

"Hell yeah, my pockets hurting anyway," Lester Jackson sputtered from the rear seat. He was seated directly behind Poppa, loading up his 380. Now Lester Jackson was special, since he was the baby brother or the brother who had got smoked earlier in the story. Goldmouth was his brother and since he had been gunned down, Lester wasn't right in the head after that. And right about now, if smoking another nigga was on the agenda, he was down with it too.

"Hey, you think these cats got some paper on them?" He asked, just as he put the last bullet in his gun.

"I don't give a fuck what they got in their pockets! Whatever it is, we jacking all of that shit today!" Freddie B said as he sat in the front seat, mental focused on doing the guys behind them dirty, real fucking dirty.

"I don't give a fuck about nothing. All I know is that I have to get back over to Belmont Heights right after this," Curtis spoke.

"Why, what's good lil' homie?" Freddie B asked as he fantasied about the lick they were all about to pull off.

"Nigga, I just cashed my grandmothers Welfare check and I know she's waiting on me, so that she can head off to Bingo."

"Oh boy! I know that's right; Ms. Fanny can be real cranky when she misses Bingo," Lester shouted, then asked. "How long before we get to the spot, Poppa?"

"We already here, my nigga. Now you niggas play this shit cool! We 'bout to smoke these niggas and leave their dead asses back here behind those raggedy ass wood houses over there," Poppa spoke as he pointed over at some run down, old wood houses.

"Damn, does anyone live in them old ass houses?" Freddie B asked as he stared over at what was about to be the last thing he ever witnessed.

Chapter 38
Whatever Happened To Them Boys?

In the car behind the four goons up ahead, there was nothing but Kush weed smoke and slow music playing inside the car with Lil' Breezy and Big Breezy. "You know these niggas up ahead has to be the dumbest niggas I have ever seen?" Big Breezy said as it seemed as if the car up ahead had pulled over to what looked like some Bandos.

"I know, right? But don't worry, I got something for that ass, you better believe it!" Lil' Breezy said as he placed the car in park.

"Where you think we at?" Big Breezy asked as his head seemed to be on a swivel as he searched his surroundings.

"Beats me. But back a few miles, I seen a sign that read, Apopka City Limits. So I would take a wild guess and assume that we're in Apopka," Lil' Breezy versed as he looked around as well.

"It don't matter though, we ain't gone be here long," Lil' Breezy continued with as he looked over at his cousin, one last time. In the distance you could hear Freddie B yelling. "Hey, she's back here, come on!"

"Now I know gotdamn well that the bitch we are looking for don't live back behind these raggedy ass houses!" Lil' Breezy said to his cousin. "You know we can turn around and get the fuck out of here?"

"Yeah we could. But then that would take the fun out of everything. Just be cool cousin, I got this," Lil' Breezy spat as he jumped out of his car, then went to the trunk. He was back there for approximately three minutes. Just enough time to do what it was he did. He then closed the trunk and ran to the passenger side of the car. "Be right back, don't you move, because when I get back, we're going to have to be out of here in a hurry," he told his cousin.

"Yeah lil' bruh, you must make sure you come back?" Big Breezy told him as he turned his feet inside his Air Jordans, the solid red and white ones.

Up ahead, every one of the guys that were inside the old school Cutlass had already disappeared behind the houses. "Just as soon as these niggas get back here, we knock their asses out! After that, we strip them niggas butt ass naked and take everything they fucking got!" Freddie B spoke with a devious smile etched on his face. Neither one of them cared that they were about to kill two men, for nothing. A simple case of senseless black on black crime, committed in the hood.

***

When I dialed Rhynyia's phone, my call was sent directly to her voicemail. Not knowing what to make out of it, I dialed the number right back. This is when I got the same results. At that moment, my mental went to spinning, with this and that. Now why isn't she answering her phone and why hasn't she called me yet? I asked myself as I stepped out of my room into the hallway. But just as I stepped into the hallway, I was met by Entyce. She had a somber look on her face.

"Hey, the girls and I were worried about you."

"Yeah. Well all is good," she uttered. "Okay, we all thought that you might have went to get rid of Reese."

What she said next left me wondering about her and Reese. "I did, shit when I found him you won't believe where them crackers had him," she said as she looked up at me.

"Where?"

"They had him held up in some nice ass houses in Sanford."

"Well let me ask you this?" I said to her right when she told me. "No, I didn't kill him. I couldn't they had too many cameras all over the place. But get this?"

"What, Entyce?"

"He says that he's not testifying to anything. He claims that whatever he knows, he's not telling it."

A disgusted look emerged onto my face. "But how sure of this can you be?"

"Trust me Mike, he claims that his lips are sealed. He said something about you being too good to him to rat us all out," she said as I could see the sincerity in her eyes. Or maybe it was just the simple fact that she still truly loved the man.

"But let me ask you something?"

"Go head."

"Is that your heart speaking or your gut feeling of what you don't want to believe?" I asked her. Not really trusting the man who could send all of us to jail for life. She was real quiet for a moment, with her back facing me. She then turned around with a lone tear snaking down her face, she said,

"Gee Mike, I really don't know. So, do you really think that he might tell?"

I exhaled the breath that was inside my lungs and replied. "Hell Entyce, you know the nigga better than I do. So that's a question for you to answer."

"There's no need to answer that, Entyce, I'll answer that for you," Tameia said as she came from out of nowhere, in her hand she carried a small thirty eight special. Her gun was still smoldering. My head went from Tameia to Entyce.

"No! No! Tameia, please tell me that you didn't do what I think you did!" Entyce shouted as she lunged out for the short Tameia.

"Yeah I did what you couldn't do! Now please don't make me do you too!" was all she uttered as she stood there, gun now pointed at Entyce.

Damn! I couldn't believe that this shit had all come down to this. Something that I would have never expected. Not now, not today, not ever.

***

Inside the lil' bucket, that those females were riding in, neither one of them knew what was up ahead in their immediate future. All they thought of was the measly lil' few dollars they thought that they were about to make.

"So Eat'em Up, how much money you plan on making?" Lil' Kitty asked from the front seat of the bucket as she chewed on a bag of Funyuns and sipped on a cold Pepsi.

"I know I need to at least make around three hundred dollars, since I have to put my lil' bad ass son in somebody's daycare this week!" She said as she sat in the back seat, eating out of her friend's bag of chips.

"I know that's right, girl. My lil' bad ass son just finished the first grade so now I have to get his lil' bad ass some school clothes," Lil' Kitty replied as she turned to look at the girls in the back seat. "So what about you, Ass." Lil' Kitty was about to call her the name that people called her behind her back but caught herself and simply asked. "So how about you, Brittany? I know you ready to go up here and do the damn thing?"

"You better believe it! As soon as we get there I'm eating up the first damn guy I see! And if his ass has some long ass Dreads, I'm eating all up in his fine ass?" She blurted out.

"Ewwww! Bitch do you have to always eat out a niggas ass? By the way, you can have that soda," Project Hoe blurted out as she sat next to her girl.

"Bitch please! I don't know why you hoes all up in this car acting like y'all are better than me! Hell, just last week Tommy Stevens told me that you and his other chick from around the way came over to his spot and ate up every nigga at they trap spot!" Brittany shouted, putting Project Hoe on blast.

"Tommy Steven's a gotdamn lie! We or should I say me did not eat in his ass! Hell, the nigga's dick was too short to even get inside this good ass pussy!" She yelled.

Ms. Ceily cut in with, "Wait one fucking minute, not my Tommy Stevens! That's my fucking baby daddy!"

"Ahh shit!" Lil' Kitty uttered.

Pooooooow!

Then the car swerved across traffic.

"Ahhh shit! What the fuck?" Ms. Ceily shouted as she wrestled with her steering wheel as she tried her best to keep her bucket from hitting any other cars. Sad to say, the chicks didn't have any insurance at all.

Chapter 39
Nothing Good Last Forever

Mignon, Nicole and Strawberry were just a few cars behind the little bucket, when Nicole noticed something up ahead. "Oh shit! What the fuck?" She shouted, this quickly woke up ole Berry, who was in the back seat, sleeping.

"What happened?" She asked as Mignon swerved to the right of the road. Her quick actions prevented them from hitting the car in front of them. "I don't know, but it looks like that lil' bucket that them hoes are riding in, just caught a flat tire!" Nicole spoke as she leaned up in her seat.

"Well I be damned!" Mignon said as she seen how the bucket swerved across traffic. They were all on Interstate 4, just passing by the Deland exit.

"Ahh man, them hoes lucky that they didn't hit anyone!" Strawberry said as she leaned up in her seat. Up front there were a bunch of cars, all stopped right there in the middle of the two-lane highway. "So what, do you guys think that we should go give them a hand or something?" she asked as she looked from Mignon to Nicole. "Hell nah, that's what Ms. Ceily gets for having them MAY POP tires on her lil' bucket."

"I know that's right," Mignon uttered as they could see Ms. Ceily and the entire car of females standing outside of the bucket, heads down looking all dejected and shit. "Now this is just what we needed for them hoes to not make it up to Jacksonville," Mignon said as they sat off to the side of the road, observing what was taking place.

"Nicole, can I please ask you, what in the hell are May Pop tires?" Strawberry asked as she sat there staring at Nicole.

"Sure, let me school your ass on something that I heard Mike's mom say one day. I guess he was trying to get some tires for cheap and when she heard him talking about them she told him not to buy those tires called, May Pop Tires."

"What is that the name brand of them or something?" Strawberry asked with a quizzical unit on her face.

"Nah girl, don't you get it? May Pop Tires is exactly what she was trying to say," Nicole uttered as she turned to look her in the face.

"What? I don't get it?" Strawberry asked as she continued to probe.

"Damn Strawberry! They're called May Pop, because that's what they do. They just might pop! Just like what happened to them silly ass hoes!" Nicole said as she pointed up ahead at the females in the bucket.

By now all sorts of people were out of their cars, trying to help assist the girls. But what had took the blunt of the near fatal accident was the bucket. When the tire burst, Ms. Ceily lost control of the car for a mere fraction of a few seconds. That's when her car slammed into the concrete barrier, now causing a great big dent in the driver side of the car. And since Keisha was sitting right behind the driver, her head bumped up against the door frame and now she was left with a big ass gash on her face.

Meanwhile, all Lil' Kitty could say was. "Damn girl! Now how we gone go up there and get this money?" She was highly upset, jumping up and down on the Interstate, acting a straight fool.

"Fuck that Lil' Kitty, look at my gotdamn car!" Ms. Ceily shouted as you could hear the sirens in the distance, approaching fast.

"Girl! Fuck that piece of shit, you call a car! What I want to know is how am I going to get to Jacksonville now, to see my boo thang, Punkin!" Lil' Kitty shouted, not one bit concerned about Ms. Ceily or her car, needless to say, the unfortunate predicament that Ms. Ceily was now left in. Lil' Kitty didn't give a flying fuck about Ms. Ceily or her car. What she cared about most was how she was going to get up to Jacksonville.

"Lil Kitty, what about the girls in the car, do you even care about them?" Lil' Kitty threw her hands up in the air, then shouted back at her.

"Not now, I have to call my boo and try to convince him to come down here, since we won't be making it up there!" She shouted as she walked off the shoulder of the road.

"Now Mignon, you know how persistent she can become when she really wants something? This lil' heifer just might be still trying to get up to Jacksonville," Nicole said as she sat in the passenger seat.

"I know, right. And I'm afraid that's probably what she's trying to do right about now, look!" Mignon said as she pointed at Lil' Kitty on the side of the road, on her phone.

"So who do you all think she's calling?" Strawberry asked as she looked at what was transpiring.

"Well it sure as hell isn't a gotdanm tow truck! That bitch is probably on the phone right now, with whomever has Punkin's phone," Nicole versed.

"I don't know who it is and don't give a fuck. All I know is that someone is going to have to call her and convince her lil' hot ass to just go lay down somewhere, or either go up to Duval and get murked, right before they get all of the vital information about us that they need," Mignon said as Strawberry sat there, thinking of what to do next.

"Hold up, I got it," she shouted.

"What Strawberry?" Nicole asked her. "I'm going to call Mike; he'll know what to do," she said as she dialed my number.

***

When I received the call from Strawberry, I was in between two heated females. One with her gun pointed directly at the other. When I saw that it was Strawberry, I knew that it had to be something wrong, since she was calling and not one of the other girls.

"You two stop it, right now!" I said to both of them.

"No Mike! If this lil' chick has went and killed my baby daddy, what do you think, that I'm about to stand here and let this shit go? How am I going to raise my seed, without a father?" Entyce shouted.

"Be cool Entyce, let me answer this call, " I told her. Tameia was still standing firm, gun pointed directly at Entyce.

"Please don't make me do you like I did your rat?" Tameia blurted out.

"Hello," I said as I answered my phone, then heard what it was that Strawberry had to tell me with both females, still standing before me, with hatred and bitterness laced inside their evil hearts. It only took a few minutes before I was telling Strawberry. "Okay, I got it Berry, in the meantime I need you ladies back here as soon as possible."

Just as I hung up, I looked back over at Tameia. "Did you really have to kill the man, Tameia?"

"I didn't kill him. I just told him that he had to get out of town, before me and the rest of The Murder Queens tracked him down and then killed him," she versed.

"Oh God! Thank you Tameia, thank you!" Entyce screamed as she ran up on her and gave her a hug. Just as they let go of each other, Tameia went inside her pocket and pulled out a small piece of paper. "Here is where he's going to relocate too." She then handed Entyce a small piece of paper. "He says that he'll be waiting for you."

Entyce read the note, then brought her head up slowly right before she uttered. "Thanks Tameia, I owe you one."

"Sure thing, Entyce. And thanks for not lunging out at me." The both of them dapped one another up, while I went to make a very important phone call. Now that that had been handled, I still needed to try and stop Lil' Kitty from making the worst mistake of her very young life. Like I said, Lil' Kitty was always in the middle of something, and what she was in the middle of right now, just might have caused the most damage of all. So I had to do what it was I had to do in order to save her life.

The Final Chapter
She's What

Poppa knew this area real good. So he instructed the guys where to be.

"Freddie B you stand right over there. When these two busta ass clowns get back here, you take their heat. Curtis, you stand your ass right there. They won't think nothing if they see me and you right here. Now Lester, you walk up on the front porch."

Lester looked around as if something was wrong. "Now what in the hell am I going to do up here?" he asked, stupid ass look on his face.

"Nigga, just stand your dumb ass up there. If them niggas get out of pocket, start blasting! And don't muthafucking stop until them niggas ain't breathing anymore."

"Cool! I can do that!" He replied just as they heard some footsteps.

Freddie B's index finger instantly went up over his thick ass lips. "Shhhhh!" was the last thing he said, because just as he took his index finger down, Lil' Breezy smoked him.

Pst-pst-pst.

Three precise rounds caught him squarely in his face and chest. The last round from the Beretta 9mm caught him directly in the middle of his large head. The poor dude was dead before his lifeless body hit the hard ground.

"Oh shit!" Poppa screamed as he tried to pull out his piece. But just as he pulled it out, Lil' Breezy had the jump on his ass.

Pst-pst-pst-pst the 9mm hissed like a mad King Cobra. Two rounds hit Poppa square in his stomach, with another one catching him on his neck. The last shot was one that actually killed him though. Lil' Breezy shot the man directly in his right eye. The bullet entered Poppa's brain in a matter of seconds. He died with his left eye still open. But this is what was so fucking odd.

Lester had his 380 pointed at the kid and could have killed him, but as we all know a damn 380 ain't shit in the middle of a fucking gun battle. Especially when this kid from Duval pulled out a gotdamn 40 Cal.

Boom-Boom-Boom

Just as the 40 Cal sounded off, Big Breezy was still seated inside the car, when he heard the cannon go off.

"Damn lil' cousin, you putting in that work!" He said as he stood quickly got out of the car, then positioned himself off to the side, just in case one of them niggas had got away.

The three shots sent Lester's light ass backwards, smashing through the wood framed Bando. "Good luck with anyone being inside that old ass house!" Lil' Breezy said as he witnessed Curtis attempting to flee. "Not today my flat footed friend!" Lil' Breezy shouted as he hit the man in the back of his right leg. Curtis fell face first in some fresh ass dog shit.

"Ahh fuck! Hey man, it wasn't my idea, it was that first nigga's bright idea to rob y'all and then send you guy's straight to hell!" He shouted as he rolled over to face the man who had just killed his partners.

"Well, by the way it looks, I won't be making that trip. You will. So when you get there, tell'em that I had other plans, my friend."

"Wait a minute! Inside my right pocket is my grandmother's cash from her Welfare check."

"Okay, so what?" Lil' Breezy said with a half smirk on his face.

"You let me go and you can have all that shit, mannnnn!" Curtis tried to bargain.

"I'm gone take that anyway my nigga!" Lil' Breezy uttered, then stood up straight and fired.

Boom-Boom-Boom

The smoke from his gun was smoldering as he smoked the man, shot the brother directly in his head, without even thinking about it. Once he made sure that the man was dead, he went inside his pockets and relieved him of everything he had. Just as he stood back up, he heard a gun click. It was Lester, the badly wounded man had somehow crawled back from inside the Bando. But when his gun jammed again, he knew that his miserable ass life was over. "Fucking piece of shit!" Lester shouted.

"I know, right?" Lil' Breezy mouthed as he walked up on the man. He was bleeding profusely from out of his mouth and coughing up blood that was coming from his open wounded stomach. This is when Lil' Breezy walked over to the man and slowly lifted his head up. He wanted to speak to the man, right before he killed him and sent him on his way.

"Is there anything else that you want to tell me before I send you where the rest of your crew is?"

"Who in the fuck are you?" Lester asked as he continued to cough up blood, hot tears now streaming down his face.

"They call Lil' Breezy. And all I wanted was to find this lil' chick who might have had something to do with my people being murked up in Duval, over the weekend. But nah, you niggas had to try and set me and my cousin up. Now look at you and your dead homies. Dead as a fucking doorknob." He then coughed up some phlegm and spit in Lester's face as he witnessed Lester desperately trying to take his last breath.

"Ahh, uggh, uggh!" He sounded as he stuttered. "The chiiiiccck yyyooouu loooookkkinng for, lives in Belmont Heights and sheeee goooees by Mo Money, ever since she joined them bitches called the Florida Hot Girls, my nigga!"

was the very last words that Lester Jackson ever said. Just as he closed his eyes for the very last time. A light drizzle of rain began to come down.

"Mo Money, huh? And she dances with them chicks that have been coming back and forth to Duval. Them bitches might just be the ones responsible for all of them gotdamn killings and shit," Lil' Breezy said to himself as he ran back out to where his cousin was. They needed to get out of there before someone saw them.

Just as Lil' Breezy got back to his car, he noticed that his cousin wasn't there. "Now where in the hell is this fool?" He said as he stepped up to the passenger side.

"Pss everything good?" He heard a voice say from out of the bushes.

"Nigga! Didn't I tell your monkey ass to stay in the car?" A disgusted Lil' Breezy asked his cousin.

"That you did, cousin but when I heard your cannon go off I thought that at least one of them fools might try to escape. And when they did I was going to pop that ass," Big Breezy mouthed as he stood up and walked over to his cousin. "Good looking out, now get your silly ass in the car."

Once they were both back inside, Lil' Breezy pulled out two ounces of weed and at least three stacks of cash. "Here, put this in the glove compartment."

"Damn, them bustas had all of that on them?" a surprised looking Big Breezy asked.

"Hell yeah! I betcha them fools won't try to jack another nigga again," Lil' Breezy stated as he started up the car.

"What happened to them fools?" Big Breezy asked.

"What do you think happened? They met up with the wrong lil' nigga, on the wrong muthafucking day! Now let's go find this bitch that they call Mo Money! Lil' Breezy uttered.

"Wait a minute, Mo Money, I think I've heard that name somewhere before," Big Breezy said.

"I know you have. That bitch dances with those girls that call themselves the Florida Hot Girls," Lil' Breezy said as he pulled off from where four dead bodies lay.

"That's right! So does this other chick, who calls herself Lil' Kitty!" Big Breezy said as Lil' Breezy 's head turned on a swivel. "What, do you know her?"

"Do I? Hell, I met her lil' fine ass a few weeks ago up in Black Magic," Big Breezy told him. "Well I guess we'll pay her lil' ass a visit as well, cousin!" Lil' Breezy spat as they both made their way through traffic, headed back to Belmont Heights in search of Mo Money and possibly Lil' Kitty's ass too.

In order to get Lil' Kitty back down to earth, I texted her ass and told her that I needed to speak with her. Something about the show we had on Wednesday night. I also told her ass that she needed to be in Orlando because I was coming through to pass out their new club badges. These were the badges that they were required to wear to get them inside any club event for the free. She in turn hit me right back, telling me that she was on the way back home.

Now that I had that taken care of, it was back to trying to get myself some much-needed rest. It had been a long, stressful day in my life as the manager of one of the most sought-after dance groups in Florida. But the rest that I so desperately needed wouldn't be coming anytime soon for me, because just as I had placed my phone down, it began to ring again. Seeing that it was my brother calling for the fifth time, I decided to pick up. Something that I wish I would have never done.

"This must be very fucking important my nigga, if you keep on calling me!" I said into my phone.

"It is, Mike. And I don't know why you didn't pick up earlier?"

"I was busy, so what's up?" I asked him as I sat up in bed.

"Well, I don't know how to tell you this, but I guess I'll just start off with. "Have you heard from the girls yet?"

"No. Have you?" I asked him as I walked over to my window to witness Mignon and the girls coming down the road. "Mike, their plane went down!" He spoke somberly as if he was choking up or something.

"What did you just say?"

"The reason you haven't heard from them is because their plane went down." There it was, he had said it. Now I knew as to why I had that fucked up feeling as if something awful had happened.

"No, no! No, not my Rhynyia! Where did it go down at and how?" I shouted back into the phone, hoping that he had all the answers to my question.

"They had to fly over the Bermuda Triangle. Something about the police were tracking them and …" his country ass was talking too slow for me.

I interrupted him and said, "Don't worry about it! I'm about to call Pierre!" I then hung up before he could say anything at all. When I dialed the number to Pierre, his phone picked up on the first ring.

"Ola, Senor?" He spoke into the phone as if nothing was wrong.

"Mr. Santiago, I just found out about Rhynyia and the plane. Have you all began a search for them yet?"

"We have Mr. Michael. And don't worry, Rhynyia has a lot of resilience inside of her. That's why she's who she is. And if I know her like I know her, she's going to make sure that their entire crew of them are safe and sound."

The entire time that he was talking to me, it sounded as if the man didn't give a fuck about her or the crew.

"I'm on the next plane over to Puerto Rico, right now!" I said.

"There's no need for that young man. Trust me, they're okay. But your brother is supposed to arrive here later this week for another supply of my product. You just worry about making sure that he doesn't fuck up my money or my precious product."

"What? Wait a minute, you are concerned about your cocaine and not your daughters?" I asked him, not afraid of him at all.

"When we find them, she shall call you. You just make sure that your brother doesn't fuck up! Goodbye, Mr. Michael," he said, then hung up.

Just as I closed my phone down, is when I heard the saddest love song ever being played over the television. It fit the moment as I sat back and really listened to what George Michael was singing. The song was none other than the classic song, *Praying for Time*. So, as I sat there, deeply listening to what he was singing. It dawned on me, if only I would have had a little more time, just maybe I could have saved her. But just like I said in the beginning… their death was inevitable.

Two days earlier, the early morning of that awful flight. Rhynyia was awakened to sheer terror. Once she was informed of what was taking place, she sprinted up to the cockpit. Miguel looked terrified. When she told him to take the plane over the Bermuda Triangle, he told her that he couldn't put them in that type of danger.

"Well if you won't, I will! Now move out of my gotdamn way!" Rhynyia shouted as she took control of the Giant Bird in the sky. Moments later, they had lost the police helicopter and thought they were in the clear, when out of nowhere came a bolt of lightning that struck one of the plane engines.

"What was that?" she shouted to a frightened Miguel over in the other seat. His head quickly went to where the loud noise had come from. When he turned around he shouted. "We just lost an engine!" Rhynyia struggled with the steering wheel of the plane, but her attempts were futile as she lost control …

To Be Continued in the next installment of The Murder Queens. Praying For Time …

Lock Down Publications and Ca$h Presents
Assisted Publishing Packages

Due to an increase in the price of services we have increased our prices. The prices below reflect the price increase as of 11/1/24.

BASIC PACKAGE $699 Editing Cover Design Formatting	UPGRADED PACKAGE $1000 Typing Editing Cover Design Formatting Upload eBooks to Amazon Upload Paperback to Amazon
ADVANCE PACKAGE $1,400 Typing Editing (line editing/content) Cover Design Formatting Copyright Registration Proofreading Upload eBooks to Amazon Upload Paperback to Amazon	LDP SUPREME PACKAGE $1,700 Typing Editing (line editing/content) Cover Design Formatting Copyright Registration Proofreading Set up Amazon Account Upload eBooks to Amazon Upload Paperback to Amazon Advertise on LDP's Amazon and Facebook Page

***Other services available upon request.
Additional charges may apply

Lock Down Publications
P.O. Box 944
Stockbridge, GA 30281-9998
Phone: 470 303-9761
Email: lockdownpublications@gmail.com

Submission Guideline

Submit the first three chapters of your completed manuscript to ldpsubmissions@gmail.com. In the subject line add **Your Book's Title**. The manuscript must be in a Word Doc file and sent as an attachment. Document should be in Times New Roman, double spaced, and in size 12 font. Also, provide your synopsis and full contact information. If sending multiple submissions, they must each be in a separate email.

Have a story but no way to send it electronically? You can still submit to LDP/Ca$h Presents. Send in the first three chapters, written or typed, of your completed manuscript to:

LDP: Submissions Dept
P.O. Box 944
Stockbridge, GA 30281-9998

DO NOT send original manuscript. Must be a duplicate. Provide your synopsis and a cover letter containing your full contact information.

Thanks for considering LDP and Ca$h Presents.

NEW RELEASES

BLOODLINE OF A SAVAGE 1,2&3
THESE VICIOUS STREETS 1,2&3
RELENTLESS GOON
RELENTLESS GOON 2
BY PRINCE A. TAUHID

THE BUTTERFLY MAFIA 1-3
BY FUMIYA PAYNE

A THUG'S STREET PRINCESS 1,2&3
BY MEESHA

CITY OF SMOKE 1& 2
BY MOLOTTI

STEPPERS 1,2&3
THE REAL BADDIES OF CHI-RAQ
BY KING RIO

THE LANE 1&2
BY KEN-KEN SPENCE

THUG OF SPADES 1,2&3
LOVE IN THE TRENCHES 2
CORNER BOY CHRONICLES
BY COREY ROBINSON

TIL DEATH 3
BY ARYANNA

THE BIRTH OF A GANGSTER 4
BY DELMONT PLAYER

PRODUCT OF THE STREETS 1&2
BY DEMOND "MONEY" ANDERSON

NO TIME FOR ERROR
BY KEESE

MONEY HUNGRY DEMONS 1,2&3
BY TRANAY ADAMS

HUNGRY FOR MONEY 1&2
BY SLIMBOS

A THUGGISH PASSION
KILLAZ ON STANDBY 1&2
LAND OF DA HOOLIGANZ 1,2&3
FRESH OFF DA PORCH
BY IRA B.

COUNTDOWN OF A KILLA 1&2
GUNS DOWN, BOTTOMS UP 1&2
SEX, MURDA AND GOD
BY LO-LIFE

THE LEVEL UP 1&2
BY LUXURY KING

FO'EVA ROLLIN' 1&2
BY ASSA RAYMOND BAKER

HUB CITY MENACE 1&2
BY J. WHITE

KILLA CREW
DYING FOR LIKES
BY ARYANNA

IF YOU CROSS ME ONCE 6
ANGEL 5
By Anthony Fields

IMMA DIE BOUT MINE 5
By Aryanna

A THUGS STREET PRINCESS 3
EMBRACING THE LOVE OF A BOSS
By Meesha

PRODUCT OF THE STREETS 3
By Demond Money Anderson

STANDING ON HER BUSINESS
BY DG SANTANA

GET IT IN SLUGS 1&2
B. STALLS

CORNER BOYS 2
By Corey Robinson

THE MURDER QUEENS 6&7
By Michael Gallon

CITY OF SMOKE 3
By Molotti

CONFESSIONS OF A DOPEBOY
By Nicholas Lock

TENDER
BY KHUFU

THA TAKEOVER
By Keith Chandler

BETRAYAL OF A G 2
By Ray Vinci

CRIME BOSS 4
By Playa Ray

Coming Soon from Lock Down Publications/Ca$h Presents

RAN OFF ON THE PLUG 2 by **PAPER BOI RARI**
STREET REDEMPTION by **TONY DANIELS**
SAVAGE FAMILY EMPIRE by **PRINCE TAUHID**
BAD BITCHES WIT' GUNZ by **DIESEL**
THE SINGLE LADIES by **DIESEL**
COKE BY THE TRUCKLOAD by **DIESEL**
PROBLEM SOLVED by **DIESEL**
TIPPIN' THE SCALES by **DIESEL**
OPPS CRY TOO by **SAYNOMORE**
A GANGSTA'S KARMA by **FLAME**

AVAILABLE NOW

RESTRAINING ORDER 1 & 2
By **CA$H & Coffee**

LOVE KNOWS NO BOUNDARIES 1-3
By **Coffee**

RAISED AS A GOON I, II, III & IV
BRED BY THE SLUMS I, II, III
BLAST FOR ME I & II
ROTTEN TO THE CORE I II III
A BRONX TALE I, II, III
DUFFLE BAG CARTEL I II III IV V VI
HEARTLESS GOON I II III IV V
A SAVAGE DOPEBOY I II
DRUG LORDS I II III
CUTTHROAT MAFIA I II
KING OF THE TRENCHES
By **Ghost**

LAY IT DOWN I & II
LAST OF A DYING BREED I II
BLOOD STAINS OF A SHOTTA I & II III
By **Jamaica**

LOYAL TO THE GAME I II III
LIFE OF SIN I, II III
By **TJ & Jelissa**

IF LOVING HIM IS WRONG…I & II
LOVE ME EVEN WHEN IT HURTS I II III
By **Jelissa**

PUSH IT TO THE LIMIT
By **Bre' Hayes**

BLOODY COMMAS I & II
SKI MASK CARTEL I, II & III
KING OF NEW YORK I II, III IV V
RISE TO POWER I II III
COKE KINGS I II III IV V
BORN HEARTLESS I II III IV
KING OF THE TRAP I II
By **T.J. Edwards**

WHEN THE STREETS CLAP BACK I & II III
THE HEART OF A SAVAGE I II III IV
MONEY MAFIA I II
LOYAL TO THE SOIL I II III
By **Jibril Williams**

A DISTINGUISHED THUG STOLE MY HEART I - III
LOVE SHOULDN'T HURT I II III IV
RENEGADE BOYS 1-4
PAID IN KARMA 1-3
SAVAGE STORMS 1-3
AN UNFORESEEN LOVE 1-3
BABY, I'M WINTERTIME COLD 1-3
A THUG'S STREET PRINCESS 1&2
By **Meesha**

CUM FOR ME 1-8
An LDP Erotica Collaboration

BLOOD OF A BOSS 1-5
SHADOWS OF THE GAME
TRAP BASTARD
By **Askari**

A GANGSTER'S CODE 1-3
A GANGSTER'S SYN 1-3
THE SAVAGE LIFE 1-3
CHAINED TO THE STREETS 1-3
BLOOD ON THE MONEY 1-3
A GANGSTA'S PAIN 1-3
BEAUTIFUL LIES AND UGLY TRUTHS
CHURCH IN THESE STREETS
By **J-Blunt**

THE STREETS BLEED MURDER 1-3
THE HEART OF A GANGSTA 1-3
By **Jerry Jackson**

WHEN A GOOD GIRL GOES BAD
By **Adrienne**

THE COST OF LOYALTY 1-3
By **Kweli**

BRIDE OF A HUSTLA 1-3
THE FETTI GIRLS 1-3
CORRUPTED BY A GANGSTA 1-4
BLINDED BY HIS LOVE
THE PRICE YOU PAY FOR LOVE 1-3
DOPE GIRL MAGIC 1-3
By **Destiny Skai**

A KINGPIN'S AMBITION
A KINGPIN'S AMBITION II
I MURDER FOR THE DOUGH
By **Ambitious**

A DOPEBOY'S PRAYER
By **Eddie "Wolf" Lee**

TRUE SAVAGE 1-7
DOPE BOY MAGIC 1-3
MIDNIGHT CARTEL 1-3
CITY OF KINGZ 1&2
NIGHTMARE ON SILENT AVE
THE PLUG OF LIL MEXICO 1&2
CLASSIC CITY
By **Chris Green**

LOVE & CHASIN' PAPER
By **Qay Crockett**

THE KING CARTEL 1-3
By **Frank Gresham**

THESE NIGGAS AIN'T LOYAL 1-3
By **Nikki Tee**

GANGSTA SHYT 1-3
By **CATO**

THE ULTIMATE BETRAYAL
By **Phoenix**

BOSS'N UP 1-3
By **Royal Nicole**

I LOVE YOU TO DEATH
By **Destiny J**

BROOKLYN HUSTLAZ
By **Boogsy Morina**

GANGSTA CITY
By **Teddy Duke**

TO DIE IN VAIN
SINS OF A HUSTLA
By **ASAD**

I RIDE FOR MY HITTA
I STILL RIDE FOR MY HITTA
By **Misty Holt**

A GANGSTER'S REVENGE 1-4
THE BOSS MAN'S DAUGHTERS 1-5
A SAVAGE LOVE 1&2
BAE BELONGS TO ME 1&2
A HUSTLER'S DECEIT 1-3
WHAT BAD BITCHES DO 1-3
SOUL OF A MONSTER 1-3
KILL ZONE
A DOPE BOY'S QUEEN 1-3
TIL DEATH 1-3
IMMA DIE BOUT MINE 1-5
By **Aryanna**

BROOKLYN ON LOCK 1 & 2
By **Sonovia**

A DRUG KING AND HIS DIAMOND 1-3
A DOPEMAN'S RICHES
HER MAN, MINE'S TOO 1&2
CASH MONEY HO'S
THE WIFEY I USED TO BE 1&2
PRETTY GIRLS DO NASTY THINGS
By **Nicole Goosby**

THE STREETS ARE CALLING
By **Duquie Wilson**

LIPSTICK KILLAH 1-3
CRIME OF PASSION 1-3
FRIEND OR FOE 1-3
By **Mimi**

TRAPHOUSE KING 1-3
KINGPIN KILLAZ 1-3
STREET KINGS 1&2
PAID IN BLOOD 1&2
CARTEL KILLAZ 1-3
DOPE GODS 1&2
By **Hood Rich**

STEADY MOBBN' 1-3
THE STREETS STAINED MY SOUL 1-3
By **Marcellus Allen**

WHO SHOT YA 1-3
SON OF A DOPE FIEND 1-4
HEAVEN GOT A GHETTO 1&2
SKI MASK MONEY 1&2
By **Renta**

GORILLAZ IN THE BAY 1-4
TEARS OF A GANGSTA 1/&2
3X KRAZY 1&2
STRAIGHT BEAST MODE 1&2
By **DE'KARI**

TRIGGADALE 1-3
MURDA WAS THE CASE 1-3
By **Elijah R. Freeman**

MARRIED TO A BOSS 1-3
By **Destiny Skai & Chris Green**

SLAUGHTER GANG 1-3
RUTHLESS HEART 1-3
By **Willie Slaughter**

GOD BLESS THE TRAPPERS 1-3
THESE SCANDALOUS STREETS 1-3
FEAR MY GANGSTA 1-5
THESE STREETS DON'T LOVE NOBODY 1-2
BURY ME A G 1-5
A GANGSTA'S EMPIRE 1-4
THE DOPEMAN'S BODYGAURD 1&2
THE REALEST KILLAZ 1-3
THE LAST OF THE OGS 1-3
By **Tranay Adams**

KINGZ OF THE GAME 1-7
CRIME BOSS 1-4
By **Playa Ray**

FUK SHYT
By **Blakk Diamond**

DON'T F#CK WITH MY HEART 1&2
By **Linnea**

ADDICTED TO THE DRAMA 1-3
IN THE ARM OF HIS BOSS
By **Jamila**

LOYALTY AIN'T PROMISED 1&2
By **Keith Williams**

FOREVER GANGSTA 1&2
GLOCKS ON SATIN SHEETS 1&2
By **Adrian Dulan**

YAYO 1-4
A SHOOTER'S AMBITION 1&2
BRED IN THE GAME
By **S. Allen**

TRAP GOD 1-3
RICH $AVAGE 1-3
MONEY IN THE GRAVE 1-3
CARTEL MONEY
By **Martell Troublesome Bolden**

TOE TAGZ 1-4
LEVELS TO THIS SHYT 1&2
IT'S JUST ME AND YOU
By **Ah'Million**

KINGPIN DREAMS 1-3
RAN OFF ON DA PLUG
By **Paper Boi Rari**

THE STREETS MADE ME 1-3
By **Larry D. Wright**

CONFESSIONS OF A GANGSTA 1-4
CONFESSIONS OF A JACKBOY 1-3
CONFESSIONS OF A HITMAN
By **Nicholas Lock**

I'M NOTHING WITHOUT HIS LOVE
SINS OF A THUG
TO THE THUG I LOVED BEFORE
A GANGSTA SAVED XMAS
IN A HUSTLER I TRUST
By **Monet Dragun**

THE MURDER QUEENS 7 | MICHAEL GALLON

QUIET MONEY 1-3
THUG LIFE 1-3
EXTENDED CLIP 1&2
A GANGSTA'S PARADISE
By **Trai'Quan**

CAUGHT UP IN THE LIFE 1-3
THE STREETS NEVER LET GO 1-3
By **Robert Baptiste**

NEW TO THE GAME 1-3
MONEY, MURDER & MEMORIES 1-3
By **Malik D. Rice**

THE LIFE OF A HOOD STAR
By **Ca$h & Rashia Wilson**

THE STREETS WILL NEVER CLOSE 1-4
By **K'ajji**

LIFE OF A SAVAGE 1-4
A GANGSTA'S QUR'AN 1-4
MURDA SEASON 1-3
GANGLAND CARTEL 1-3
CHI'RAQ GANGSTAS 1-4
KILLERS ON ELM STREET 1-3
JACK BOYZ N DA BRONX 1-3
A DOPEBOY'S DREAM 1-3
JACK BOYS VS DOPE BOYS 1-3
COKE GIRLZ
COKE BOYS
SOSA GANG 1&2
BRONX SAVAGES
BODYMORE KINGPINS
BLOOD OF A GOON
By **Romell Tukes**

CREAM 2-3
THE STREETS WILL TALK
By **Yolanda Moore**

CONCRETE KILLA 1-3
VICIOUS LOYALTY 1-3
By **Kingpen**

THE ULTIMATE SACRIFICE 1-6
KHADIFI
IF YOU CROSS ME ONCE 1-5
ANGEL 1-4
IN THE BLINK OF AN EYE
By **Anthony Fields**

NIGHTMARES OF A HUSTLA 1-3
BLOOD AND GAMES 1&2
By **King Dream**

HARD AND RUTHLESS 1&2
MOB TOWN 251
THE BILLIONAIRE BENTLEYS 1-3
REAL G'S MOVE IN SILENCE
By **Von Diesel**

MOB TIES 1-7
SOUL OF A HUSTLER, HEART OF A KILLER 1-3
GORILLAZ IN THE TRENCHES
By **SayNoMore**

BODYMORE MURDERLAND 1-3
THE BIRTH OF A GANGSTER 1-4
By **Delmont Player**

FOR THE LOVE OF A BOSS 1&2
By **C. D. Blue**

KILLA KOUNTY 1-5
By **Khufu**

MOBBED UP 1-4
THE BRICK MAN 1-5
THE COCAINE PRINCESS 1-10
STEPPERS 1-3
SUPER GREMLIN 1-4
By **King Rio**

MONEY GAME 1&2
By **Smoove Dolla**

A GANGSTA'S KARMA 1-4
By **FLAME**

KING OF THE TRENCHES 1-3
By **GHOST & TRANAY ADAMS**

QUEEN OF THE ZOO 1&2
By **Black Migo**

GRIMEY WAYS 1-3
BETRAYAL OF A G
By **Ray Vinci**

XMAS WITH AN ATL SHOOTER
By **Ca$h & Destiny Skai**

KING KILLA 1&2
By **Vincent "Vitto" Holloway**

BETRAYAL OF A THUG 1&2
By **Fre$h**

THE MURDER QUEENS 1-6
By **Michael Gallon**

FOR THE LOVE OF BLOOD 1-4
By **Jamel Mitchell**

HOOD CONSIGLIERE 1&2
NO TIME FOR ERROR
By **Keese**

PROTÉGÉ OF A LEGEND 1&2
LOVE IN THE TRENCHES 1&2
By **Corey Robinson**

THE PLUG'S RUTHLESS DAUGHTER 1&2
By **Tony Daniels**

BORN IN THE GRAVE 1-3
CRIME PAYS 1&2
By **Self Made Tay**

MOAN IN MY MOUTH
By **XTASY**

TORN BETWEEN A GANGSTER AND A
GENTLEMAN
By **J-BLUNT & Miss Kim**

HERE TODAY GONE TOMORROW 1&2
By **Fly Rock**

PILLOW PRINCESS
By **S. Hawkins**

SANCTIFIED AND HORNY
by **XTASY**

WOMEN LIE MEN LIE 1-4
FIFTY SHADES OF SNOW 1-3
STACK BEFORE YOU SPLURGE
GIRLS FALL LIKE DOMINOES
NAÏVE TO THE STREETS
By **ROY MILLIGAN**

LOYALTY IS EVERYTHING 1-3
CITY OF SMOKE 1&2
By **Molotti**

THE BUTTERFLY MAFIA 1-4
SALUTE MY SAVAGERY 1&2
By **Fumiya Payne**

THE LANE 1&2
By **Ken-Ken Spence**

THE PUSSY TRAP 1-5
By **Nene Capri**

DIRTY DNA
By **Blaque**

BOOKS BY LDP'S CEO, CA$H

TRUST IN NO MAN
TRUST IN NO MAN 2
TRUST IN NO MAN 3
BONDED BY BLOOD
SHORTY GOT A THUG
THUGS CRY
THUGS CRY 2
THUGS CRY 3
TRUST NO BITCH
TRUST NO BITCH 2
TRUST NO BITCH 3
TIL MY CASKET DROPS
RESTRAINING ORDER
RESTRAINING ORDER 2
IN LOVE WITH A CONVICT
LIFE OF A HOOD STAR
XMAS WITH AN ATL SHOOTER